Helen Flint was born in C...
1952 and educated at Da...
University and Oxford. She spent her
childhood on the move between the
USA, Nigeria, Canada and the UK.

She has worked as kitchen crew on the
Ferry which crosses the legendary Bay
of Fundy, a schoolteacher of English,
Drama and Russian, a translator/
abstractor for an art publisher, and is
currently a bogey-person in the guise
of an examiner for the expiring GCE.

Now living in Bournemouth, she is
married and has two small children.

Author's Note
The fictional AIR CANADA
featured in this book bears no
resemblance to the actual AIR
CANADA.

Return Journey

Helen Flint

BLACK SWAN

To Billie

RETURN JOURNEY

A BLACK SWAN BOOK 0 552 99319 0

Originally published in Great Britain by
William Heinemann Ltd.

PRINTING HISTORY
William Heinemann edition published 1987
Black Swan edition published 1988

This book is set in 11/12 pt Mallard
by Colset Private Limited, Singapore.

Black Swan Books are published by
Transworld Publishers Ltd., 61–63
Uxbridge Road, Ealing, London W5 5SA, in
Australia by Transworld Publishers
(Australia) Pty. Ltd., 15–23 Helles Avenue,
Moorebank, NSW 2170, and in
New Zealand by Transworld Publishers
(N.Z.) Ltd., Cnr. Moselle and Waipareira
Avenues, Henderson, Auckland.

Made and printed in Great Britain by
The Guernsey Press Co. Ltd.,
Guernsey, Channel Islands.

1 On the Edge

My mother had been issued with a one-way ticket to
Hell; she never travels alone. She can't: she needs assistance every inch of the way.

The majority of the strangers under the dome of the
Main Building at Halifax Airport, Nova Scotia, check in
their luggage at the counter emblazoned with a red
maple leaf and wander about independently, looking
into the shallow shop-front mock-ups and boutiques
along the vast indoor lanes. But there is always someone
in a wheelchair. Perhaps you notice this? You could not
say *who*, for, like the man who robs a bank wearing
a hearing-aid, the device camouflages the person. Only a
whisper of rubber on marble hums nearer, squeaks
round a corner and disappears. If you glance round, you
only do so to see if there *are* legs beneath the tartan
blanket.

My mother is about to assume her camouflage outside
the airport but there is a hitch. There is always a hitch.
Arnold is the hitch: her brother-in-law and my uncle. He
is trying to lift the wheelchair from the boot of his small
blue Ford Anglia. It is a heavy contraption, inaptly
called an 'Everest', and was awkwardly jammed in
there in the first place. He is unused to the physical
struggle, though the metaphysical ones have made him
pale, tubby, nondescript, myopic, uneasy. With every
difficult theological wrangle, he has grown an inch
shorter, a pound heavier, a shade whiter.

He is afraid he will have to hug the chair to his white

shirt and spoil it. I hope he does. The wheel is trapped on the jack; I put it there and felt it snap into a locked embrace with the spring. He gazes for a moment at his reflection in the enormous automatic glass doors and consults his watch. I see all this through the rearview mirror, sitting, waiting, amused.

My mother's window in the front is open; it is hot August, so hot that the tyres are melting into the tarmac and flies are falling exhausted against the windscreen.

'Vorrgodssaykgeddamoovom' – out of her window, and loud enough to embarrass him.

'I'll have to go and help him, Mum.' One of her arms drifts up over her head and I retrieve it, and put it back on her lap. The gesture moves her. She smiles.

For to whom shall Arnold appeal for help? Uncertainty, like a small loss of faith, is puffing his puffed cheeks. I see through the mirror the new beads of sweat. Uniformed boys are lurking with grins beneath their caps but he knows, should he beckon them through the glass doors, out of the air-conditioning into the heat, his own wife, twitching next to me in the back of the car, would chastise him for 'not being able to do a simple thing . . .'

And he should have to tip them: not that he is mean; it is the social transaction he fears, the mathematics involved, and the possibility of failure and ridicule.

So it is me, is it not, Arnold? The one who put the damned thing there in the first place. But how anxious you feel in my presence: at risk. As if I thought about you with a perception untinged with love or avuncular respect.

I push past Arnold; he is used to being ignored, scorned, spat upon, and, grasping the wheel-rods, free the chair and lift it clear in one movement. As it hits the tarmac it opens, the wings of its grey vinyl arms sticky with heat, wet and membranous. It shakes and hovers there a moment on the black floor, a damp, grey bat about to take flight. A kick here, a jerk there, willy-nilly apparently, to stiffen its folds into a vehicle, a means of transport.

'Aye-noshdaying ear awlday . . .' my mother is saying, buzzing and flapping in the front seat.

6

'Of course you're not staying here all day. We've got things to do, planes to catch.' I point out the luggage on the roof-rack to Arnold, as one would to a native bearer possessed of no English. He wilts. Perhaps it is the heat?

The uniformed boys, having seen the wheelchair, have abandoned their grins and come through the glass doors unbidden, to help. Now you have sherpas, Arnold, you'll manage.

'What was it, darling, I couldn't . . .' Gloria is saying to my mother, her sister, 'I couldn't quite . . . It's the noise of those blessed insects, I can't . . .' My mother is saying to her that she does not want a stranger to push her chair: they go too fast and are not sensitive.

But all Gloria hears is 'eyedonewanthomen inunorm do push' and tries to lift her out of her seat at an awkward angle, hoping that reaction might be relevant.

'NO!'

It is the one and only clear syllable my mother can speak. No wonder it is a child's first. Gloria recoils, hurt. Only I must lift her, no one else. Gloria has tended her, loved her, for years; I have come suddenly to take her back to England, years of neglect, so many we do not even speak of it, and only I am allowed to lift her.

But Gloria never wilts, she stiffens. Life is hard. Though she was spared *this*, life is harder for her, in fact.

How fragile my mother is: no more than five stone, so thin her skeleton is almost external. She barely dents the ribbed sweat-seat of the front passenger side. She barely weighs in the arms. But breakable, friable. She smells of urine and scented face-wipes. It is not her fault. Nothing is her fault. Flies rush up off the liquid tarmac. An audience of maroon-capped boys watch, holding the luggage, waiting. My mother sees them, her face twisting into contempt.

'Whaathey loogyad?'

'They are looking at us and our marvellous beauty dazzles them. Put your arms around my neck, can you?' I

7

only say 'can you' every so often so that, in case she does, by accident, it will seem to have been an achievement. Everyone needs achievements, especially those for whom achievements are out of the question. Those who can take no steps must be reminded that they are making no false ones.

Of course, she cannot. Cannot aim them so exactly, arms or legs, or even eyes. It is a wonder that she saw the boys, that peripheral vision encompassed them in random sweep. I have to fish for the arms inside the hot air of the car, trap them, and wind them around my neck. It is a prickly and painful embrace. She cannot moderate the hug and it tightens despite her. The smell is powerful. Her bony head, the black hair permed for the occasion, but now standing in tufts at the back, as a baby's does from lying too long in one position, rests against my collar-bone, bruising it. Her long nails, painted tomato-red for the occasion, are digging into the back of my neck. I stoop and scoop her lower half up with a hand under her knees, only a few inches deep, and swing her into the chair a few feet from the car door which barely registers the change from supplicant and empty to occupied.

Gloria is busy, busy, busy, retrieving packets from the back of the car, as if she wouldn't have had time to lift her sister, as if she had not wanted to anyway. She has labelled packets for me. I am strapping my mother into the chair, arranging the wayward arms down on her lap, avoiding the barbed wire of her hands.

'Here, you might need these.' She smiles.

'What do you mean?' Gloria asks me, finally emerging.

'Just a joke. Meant she might need her hands.'

'I thought you meant these packets, Jane. Some things are not funny. Your mother . . .' It is not in the distortion of speech alone that communication runs aground, I see, for Aunty and I speak the same language, so I am told. Arnold, of course, thinks in Latin, so we may excuse him.

'Since tempus fugit, Uncle,' I say unto him, in order to perk up his flagging eyelids somewhere in the distant spiral behind those thick glasses, 'let us take advantage of the "Disabled" sticker and leave the car here?'

'Yes, if your mother doesn't mind?'

'Whyyonerfshullayemine?' she asks, puzzled. What Arnold is suffering from now might be pre-guilt for all the times he will be tempted (though not succumb, I'm sure) to take advantage of the sticker when she is no longer with them.

'Waymydugs?' she suddenly shouts at her sister.

'What did she say, Jane?'

I start to push the chair away up the ramp towards the sherpas. For Christ's sake, why can't she understand her, after all this time? And I, away for years, still can?

'She said, where are her drugs?' I call out from the top of the ramp, at the top of my voice, to her dismay.

It was part of my mother's character to 'call a spade a spade': a type of aggression, so she was never known to refer to anything as 'medicine' or 'tablets'. Drugs are drugs: let's face it.

'Ah, don't worry dear,' Gloria pants at my mother at the glass doors, 'I have all the medication here, all the different things. It will all become clear. I'm going to explain it all to Jane.'

Silly Mummy. You forgot people in wheelchairs are idiots, especially those with distorted speech. Still, there is in her sad survey of the packets presented for her inspection an awareness blessedly absent from the idiot that none of these drugs even pretend to have curative powers.

Gloria explains all the ironies of this medication: for example how she must take the contraceptive pill every day so that she does not have periods, which would kill her. She, the last person in the world who needs contraception. A strange interference in the female nature, for surely if periods would kill my mother – gently, naturally, mercifully perhaps, should they not be allowed to do so?

9

Gloria does not hear her saying 'rubbish' over and over again, while the drugs are being explained, under her breath, but I do and keep it to myself. Why, I don't know. For the sake of peace, and a Good Parting.

We must have a Good Parting. I know that my mother will never see Gloria again. Arnold doesn't count. But these two are sisters after all. There is another sister, Barbara. Where is she? I wonder. This is not the time nor the place to ask.

The light inside the airport is uniform, unnatural. Arnold is away checking in luggage, nodding and acquiescing by a weighing-machine, pointing over to our group where we are arranged near a coffee machine which offers seven permutations of brown liquid. Gloria and I are standing on either side of the chair, the Good Angel and the Bad. But which is which? My mother is rocking gently, against the strap holding her, humming a tune perhaps. She loves to travel, loves arriving, new beginnings.

Gloria is anxious, twitching. She is thin from chain-smoking and her skin yellow-brown from too long in New Zealand years ago. She is nervous, taut, on the edge.

It is my mother who deserves to be mad, blessedly mad, and is not; and Gloria who should be sane, and is not. Unless, being objective (which is not possible) you could say that since my mother is unable to have a consistent and reasonable view of the world, she too is mad.

It is not merely my opinion. Many people say relatives of theirs are mad: 'my mad aunt' is almost an affectionate appellation. Not here, though. Three doctors, one of them a psychiatrist, agree with me. Her hair, once a mousy brown with a hint of Nanny's red-gold, turned grey at the temples, presumably where they put the jump-lead electrodes for her 'etceteras' as she calls them.

There is no longer any stigma attached to mental illness. Let us be modern about it, my mother begged everyone. It is like a broken leg, no worse. A broken

10

mind. Being put into traction. Think of it like that. Gloria will be cured, because a broken mind can be glued back together, fused back together, with electrodes.

It worked too. She is completely cured; she no longer believes herself to be radioactive, no longer has communications from the Halifax Naval base through her earrings, no longer obtains shotguns (all too available here in North America) to point at Arnold when he removes the protective tin-foil from the furniture in their house. My brother's comment, when he heard of this escapade, was simply 'if only she'd been a better shot!' We are not a sentimental pair, my bro and I.

But still there *is* something wrong. If she gets a static shock from a doorknob, her face goes blank. And sometimes there is a little stupidity in her, where she was quick, witty, avian. It has slowed her down, the fusing.

Of course, what she needed, my uneducated grandmother once remarked, was simply *someone to talk to.* Over the years since her death, I have come to understand this simple and wise remark.

Gloria the Glorious and Good Angel, with her ladderless nylons and the handbag which matches her shoes.

You don't fool me. Don't you find purity turns once again to madness, Gloria, lying there in the unshared double bed with him, a one-time Catholic priest with whom you may not enjoy the comforts of married sex, for fear of excommunication? That was the deal: you might stay in the Church, especially if far away in the Antipodes, but not in the Land of the Sane. Make your choice. Though surely desire has failed by now: failed ever to have had expression, and simply died? Surely it has. Please God, let desire have failed, not increased.

What would have been madness, would be to have endured it all with sanity. Not that there is anything so comforting about sanity: I would wish its remnants away from my mother.

* * *

11

Arnold is approaching. He has managed to manage in the real world, and is proud of himself. Some statement is lost up into the dome above us, lost in the Airport acoustics, entangled in the French Canadian droning of the public address.

He hands me boarding passes, being careful that our hands do not touch.

'Jane, what do you look like?' Gloria, on the other hand, is trying to touch me, to straighten me up. She wants to make some contact. My grandmother might have said, all she needs is someone to touch. Not me, no sir. There is no need to withdraw, though. There won't be any static between us: we are both Bad Angels.

The answer is 'like myself, Aunty': twenty-six years old, short, with long fair hair (unbrushed), one hundred and ten pounds, as the Canadians would say, for they seem to be able to quantify one like so much ground beef for the freezer at a glance. And wearing what? This is the root of her criticism, and it is only a ritual thought, a Fused Thought: jeans. And leather sandals over bare brown feet (washed this morning in a hotel sink) and a shirt with a blue and white check. Sensible outfit, don't you think, for this great expedition?

'My best jeans, which cannot be laddered, which will not rise up with a small draught coming up a gangplank, which will absorb an amazing amount of splashed duty-free liquor without giving evidence of it. You can put things in them too: small change, a boarding pass, a lighter, a ticket to ride, a watch that's not waterproof' – a fatal dose of Mogadon, a gun. I smooth down the Levis as if they were Vanderbilt. Attitude is everything.

Embarrassed at the turn of the conversation, Arnold is looking up at the dome above us. He feels outnumbered.

'Fine piece of architecture' he says, and he is not entitled to Fused Thoughts like that.

'Thank you, Uncle' Mummy laughs, looking at the smoothed thighs, for nothing pleases her like seediness, like slightly poor taste.

We move over to the Boarding Terminal. Gloria is

trying to give us a box of chocolates – milk chocolates. Neither of us want or like them in the least. She must have known this. She does know this. Which half of the brain forgot? Terminal Boarding. Arnold is glazing over, out of it, pretending to concentrate on the announcements. Could that be a slightly incorrect use of the Gerund?

And I am listening to Gloria. Trying to. What is she saying now? I find her harder to understand than my mother, who slurs her speech. It is aphorism, by which she has had to lead her life. Everything has a beginning, middle and end; enough is as good as a feast; every cloud has a silver dog who has its day, or tide, or way, for new brooms . . . and we must count our blessings (minus one, minus two) and Do Our Best and Be A Sport, for there are lights at the ends of tunnels, and things are Not what they Seem, and sometimes –

My grandmother, Nanny, started all this, all these antimnemonics which represent the hardships of life skated over, passed over, forgotten; only hers were more poetic, more surrealistic. Wild geese never laid tame eggs. What does a tame egg do? Go for walks with you? My Nan could ride to Jericho on That Lip, or spot a Red-Hat-No-Drawers a mile away. A bad workman quarrelled with his tools: 'Look here, hammer . . .' Good wine needed no bush: 'Well! What's this privet doing in my glass?'

A bad workman was hammering the bushes out of the wine with the dog at his heels just as a silver cloud blocked the end of the tunnel, when someone announced, to save us from the descending sweep of a giant New Broom:

'Will those recrying bording ashishtanche . . .' The girl on the tannoy sounds like my mother. Perhaps we are hearing my mother through a loudspeaker turned down? How the Hell are they going to give us Bording Ashishtanche? How will they get her into that plane? I wonder, who have trouble putting her into a car . . .

Gloria has started to weep now. Oh God, we are

13

having it all, are we? She is shaking, positively radio-active. Arnold looks grave, in the presence of such apparently raw emotion. Are we having a Good Parting? Hard to say.

'Oh, Charlie!' she throws herself into the wheelchair where she pinions the waving arms into an embrace as painful as the one my mother is no doubt giving her back. They scuffle, they scrum. Gloria emerges with a red leathery face, and a scratch down her neck. Arnold bends and places a small dry kiss on her cheek, wet with his wife's. Do you suppose this is the closest they ever come to kissing each other?

I kiss neither of them. I have not yet learnt the hypocrisy, but I will. They don't expect it. Gloria is already stiffening. Life is hard. Nieces don't love you. Arnold has on the face of a frustrated bishop. The desire to kiss his ring passes rapidly, aided by the fact of his not wearing one.

A stewardess is waiting for us by the doors out to the runway at the bottom of the ramp. Over my shoulder I can see Gloria drowning in the plate glass up above, waving as she goes down, or seems to go down as we recede. Arnold is praying to himself. The strength of the sunlight on the glass obliterates their images. What will become of them now they have no one to pity? Will they at last take pity on themselves?

2 The Winching

The stewardess is perfumed with Lily of the Valley, powdered with Yardley; pink orchid lipstick makes a perfect smile, the one reserved for idiots and children, which she is giving to my mother now. Save it, dear. Here I am pushing tragedy across the tarmac, as smooth as the cake of your foundation, to your aeroplane, and you smile the smile for idiots.

Her stomach is too discreet: surely a roll-on? A requirement of the job: the employee shall at all times be of flat tummy and shelf-breasts. Her buttocks resist and relax as she walks to the side of the Everest.

'Shall I . . .?' she begins, addressing me. Here we go.

'My mother speaks English' I interrupt, rudely. She bends, the buttocks spreading momentarily into every stretchy inch of the maroon skirt, to speak to my mother. Her breasts swell off their cross-your-heart shelf towards my mother. Her white blouse is newly-white, her hair newly-blonde and pinned into a French bun, assisted by a hair-piece the size of a salami. We can't have stray hairs in the airline dinners.

'Shall I put you in the middle of the plane, where you will have more space?' An odd question, since our seats are numbered on the boarding passes.

'Ayedonewannabewayeschaepehattis foruddersmussbablegeddout firss!' The stewardess looks up at me, perplexed, frightened. For a moment it seems as if the plastic calm required of employees at all times is crumbling a little.

'Do we have a kah-munication prah'blem?'

'You do. My mother understands you perfectly.'

'I'm not shirr what she said.' Go on, make a wild guess.

'She doesn't want to be near an escape hatch where she might prevent others getting out quickly in the event of an emergency.'

'Oh, I'm shirr there will be no such emergency,' she says, turning from me to my mother at the last minute, remembering. Her smile now is not at all convincing, a smile for sceptics, a smile for theologians who have put a difficult question to one of great faith.

Without warning, as the stewardess is still walking by the chair, about half way to the plane, my mother swings her left arm out in an arc and wallops the dear little dolly-bird soundly on the roll-on. She doubles up, more out of surprise than pain. I push the chair quickly forward in case she retaliates from instinct. But of course, she has none, or those she had have been removed at Stewardess School. Employees are required to react according to preordained patterns laid down by the Company.

Just as well.

'She can't help it. I should stand clear.' I ought to have buckled the tapes more securely.

Can't help it, I can see her French bun thinking as she walks faster, why can't she? Blind people don't hit you; paraplegics don't suddenly punch you. Why should disability be so violent? How can she fathom it?

We are nearly there. By 'there' I mean not so much at the aeroplane as under it. It seems to be several miles in the air. Most passengers never have this view of the vehicle; only the men who supply the fuel, check the undersides of the wings.

A lift descends from the cockpit. Are they going to put her in the cockpit? When the lift reaches the tarmac, it is three inches clear of the ground. My mother is shaking, but her face maintains a polished smile, the one reserved for idiots and children. A dark man in green

16

overalls several sizes too small, takes over. He has, everywhere but where Adam had his, a maple leaf. He is like a black bear clothed for a joke, who, being friendly, has decided to join in with the joke.

'Madam,' he grins down at my mother, taking both her hands in his, as if he has been doing this for her once a week for a year. Here we are again, Madam. The smile on her face changes, softens. After all, this man ignored me, not her.

'There is no need t'be skerred. I usda be middle-weight champeen of New Brunswick, and I'm gonna liftya, and this 'ere contrapshin, onto this platform. We'll take a ride together up into the cockpit.' Ah, not me, it seems. My mother looks round with panic in her eyes. It is this gesture rather than her gasped 'my-dore' which the man in green interprets.

'Sorry, sorry – no can do! Inshirrance, see? But I'm yer man – lean on me.' While saying this, he lifts her and the chair onto the metal ramp and locks on the brakes. I never saw such anguish on her face before, grateful though I am for the manner of this man, for the generosity of his speech, and for the way he is stroking her shoulder with his free hand, while giving the signal, a nod of his head, for the ascent of the Everest to begin.

'It's alright, Mum. Close your eyes! I'll be up there waiting for you.' And I run round to the steps where passengers are now boarding, dragging all the packets and parcels that had been hooked onto the wheelchair with me. The stewardess is trying to stop me, shouting. She can't. I'm running with an urgency she cannot match, and sandals make better time than high heels. If my mother is too terrified, her breathing will go out of phase and she might asphyxiate. I have to be there at the top.

Pushing past men in Bermuda shorts with elderly mothers, ladies with small babies strapped to their fronts and backs, people with crutches – all the halt, lame, walking-wounded, elderly, young, encumbered, who are being given the privilege of early boarding – I push and shove until I am at the top. I duck under the outstretched arm of a copy of the first stewardess and a man and run down the empty aisle of the plane into First Class, where it says Do Not Enter, and on into the cockpit, through a long curtain, an incongruous curtain like those which old ladies in England put behind their front doors to stop draughts penetrating.

They are pulling the Everest into the cabin, over a small lip at the door. Beyond the open door is a sickening drop, the view a parachutist gets just before it is his turn to step up to the threshold. Beyond the ramp are the flashing blue lights of Airport Security zigzagging across the tarmac.

Her lips are turning blue.

The air is thick, hot, and smells of fuel.

'Don't hold your breath. Breathe!' and I give her an almighty thump on the chest, blowing at her nose to make her take a deep breath. Everyone there, about five men in all, jerk forwards in astonishment at this attack. One of them, perhaps seeing the blue lips, puts the transparent plastic nose-cone of an oxygen mask into my right hand. A slight hissing is coming from it. Holding it over her nose and mouth I can see the lips returning to red underneath as she finally takes a few small difficult breaths, her chest moving up and down by her own volition, not automatically.

'Good girl. Good. Sorry, Mum, they should have turned you towards the plane so you couldn't see the drop.' And I should have suggested it. No one wants to take the mask back from me, as if it is contaminated, or transformed. Perhaps it is the first time it has been used, an omen of bad luck?

Airport Security have me in the Galley, frisk me thoroughly and open all the packets which I had dropped at random as I raced through the then empty cabins. They ask me to explain all the bags and parcels, and the nature of each and every drug I am carrying. I am not in the least distressed by this sort of attention, and even

18

the threat of having to 'detain' me while the drugs are examined and the Everest taken apart, doesn't faze me. My mother's condition is so extreme, so rare, so inexplicable, that it makes me *safe*. It puts me outside the parameters of normal existence, where traffic wardens will give a ticket despite protests, where broken merchandise in a shop has to be paid for, where insult and injury are actionable. Pour on your threats and disapproval – they will get you nowhere; you have only to look at her, to take it in, and you will be struck dumb, you will apologize.

'We would like to extend our apologies to your mother . . .'

'Yes, yes. Can I go now?' God Himself will stand there at the Pearly Gates eventually, saying 'We would like to extend our apologies to you: it's all been a terrible cock-up. We are so sorry, me and the angels.'

By the time I join my mother at the back of the plane, she is very agitated, I note with satisfaction. I am pleased that she is still frightened by what seem to be threats to her well-being, since this presupposes that she has some sense of well-being to refer to. She feared she would have to make the journey alone it seems, unable to communicate her needs, and the only interpreter in the world, me, gone.

She is looking around her wildly, wide-eyed, half-critical of those settling themselves in the surrounding seats, and half-questioning. As if she might at any moment recognize someone from her distant past, as if the very person she had been waiting for all her life might appear. There's something appallingly excited about her; her movements are quite deranged in the effort to swivel and see better.

And then she turns back. She is still waiting for an explanation. Of course. I explain. But she is weary and bored, as if I am only retelling some old lie. I begin to doubt the truth of what I am saying myself and trail off.

She is upset that I caused fuss and delay, not that I

19

risked arrest to be there when she needed me. This rings a bell somewhere in the scar-tissue of adolescence.

People are being ritually welcomed behind us, and then wind their way past us to their seats. I had decided days ago, on my flight from London, that we should sit at the rear of the plane, as near the toilets as possible. We are, as it happens, next to one of the escape-hatches. What an irony that would be: Mummy first down the chute, perhaps the only one to reach safety from a burning plane, but unable to run for cover of the jungle, unable to move away as the plane exploded. Jungle? In the middle of the Atlantic?

She is saying that I must fasten her seat belt and she did not want any more of 'that gas', it made her dizzy and when could she have a drink?

What a kindness it would be simply to open the hatch over the Atlantic and shoot her out.

'It was not gas. It was oxygen and you needed it. But you won't need it again unless you are silly and hold your breath.' Why do I talk to her as if she is a child? I deserve to be told that oxygen *is* a gas and she did not *decide* to hyperventilate.

I fasten the seat-belts. Her stomach, swathed in a polyester suit of the most revolting turquoise, is nearly flush with the back of the seat. Has she lost her organs? Have they shrunk? How could I have emerged from so small a space? Or my huge brother, more to the point? Under her ribs, she is about the depth of a coffee cup.

'Mummy, if you think your arm might wave out into the aisle, when someone is coming, or the drinks trolley, you had better let me know.' Tears stand in her eyes and she looks up at the air-conditioning nipple on the dashboard above us with a haughty expression. 'I know it's not your fault. But you might hurt yourself.'

A stupid thing to say. As if someone so on the edge of existence could worry about hurting themselves. Like telling someone to put antiseptic cream on a small cut when a nuclear bomb has just exploded in the vicinity.

* * *

20

The plane starts up its engines. I hold, reluctantly, the bony claw which gropes for mine, on my lap. The plane begins to wander across the tarmac, seemingly without purpose. Trees to the East, then trees to the West, trees to the North and South. We won't glimpse the sea until we incline away from this long patch in the forest. This is Canada: simply a long patch of civilization cutting through a forest from coast to coast.

Then something poetic comes in gasps from beside me, her breathing falling and resurging, like the engines, as if to convince me that the edge of existence is a moving place to be. She says that this is her last ever journey: fifty years to travel from England to England via three continents.

I am moved. I feel sick as the plane revs and revs beneath me. All the fans and vents and pressure-nozzles whirr, the wings shudder and the air thickens. The stewardesses and the steward sit and strap themselves in. The pilot, adopting a slightly better version of my mother's speech, informs us in Canadian English and then poor French where we are going and at what cruising altitude, as if he had just decided. I wish he would concentrate on the driving. As if we didn't know. Oh, Gander and Heathrow, is it? Fancy that; I thought I might go to Bombay.

'You will make another journey, I know you will.' My head is pressed into the plastic-coated headrest, my eyes are dry and my ears already hurt.

I only want to go to Lourdes, she says, nowhere else.

And as the runway runs away, falls away, disappears and the blue grey of the sea flows under us, I cry to myself, my head turned away from her, looking out of the porthole at the Eastern Seaboard dropping away.

3   Golden Slumbers

Has anyone in the History of Man yet flown to Canada from London for a weekend for purely personal reasons? I have. Unique. I could have stayed for three weeks, the ticket allowed it. But a weekend was all I required.

All I could bear.

When you have only been married for one week, it is hard, let us say impossible, to leave your new husband for three weeks. A weekend is hard enough. She will have to be told. And told in some manner, skilful and wily, so that she may not immediately form the impression that the marriage was hurried so that she could not possibly attend and spoil it.

But even in her diminished state she has a way of getting at the truth. Or the truth simply ambushes her whether she will or no.

This is not my idea, this Return. It is hers, and Gloria's. She needs to be in England, and since she is confined to a nursing home anyway, what difference does it make? She would see me at least, she would have me in the same country – almost the same county. The idea appals me. It is the last thing I want. Parents don't usually hound you across continents. You think if there is all the water of the Atlantic between you, you are safe. But money makes a nonsense of the distance, and all too soon you are swamped, feebly whining into the darkness, 'What have I done to deserve this?'

'Won't it be nice to have your mother with you; where

you can keep an eye on her?' – thus the matron of the Halifax Nursing Home greeted me when I went to collect her. It was a direct challenge.

'I'm sure the care you have given her is unequalled in the Old Country' I had said. Let her think on that. To take the statement at its face value, how nice . . . would be to assume either that the matron and her staff were bereft of ears, eyes, feelings, etc, or that we were talking about some other patient, someone else's nice mother.

Nice is not the word, Matron. Nice is never the word with me; I hate the word.

I am just the escort back to the Heimat, a country she has not seen for eight years. And how many years would she last there? Indefinitely, they said. There is nothing fatal, nothing merciful, about her illness. She is terminally ill without hope of a terminus.

The plane is levelling off, with a deal of sighing, unbuckling and lighting up of cigarettes. The stewardess my mother walloped trips down the aisle to begin her little drama. To begin her mime of the no-such emergency which will never arise.

Brave, really, when you think of the risk. Suppose the voice-over person began a rendition of Teddy Bear's Picnic instead? Would she start to tippy-toe through imaginary woods with her life-jacket on? Would she put on the oxygen mask like a tired little teddy bear?

She removes her jacket to reveal a fine pair, the better to demonstrate the cross-strapping of the orange life-jacket.

See, Mummy, all you have to do is slip it gently over your head, find the buckles, buckle them up (it must be fifteen years since you were able to buckle anything – what fun it will be!); then find that little tittie with the red bit on, to inflate it. Don't pull anything else – you might explode. Meanwhile, you carefully place the plastic mask with rubber edging (it won't smudge your make-up, thank God) over your nose (not your throat or ears, that's it, it'll only take an hour or two) to breathe 'that gas' again. And just think, the average person only takes fifty seconds to do it. It should take you about a week, I think. But of course I'll be here to help you. When I've done my own, make no mistake: I have my priorities. Oh, the crash position, that's good. Head between the knees. No, don't try it like they are, Mum; you'll go into spasm and never sit up again.

Thank you, melons, for such an amusing display. Ah, yes, and now the escape-hatches. She points to my mother for one of them. You won't *run*, will you Mum; you have to *walk* not run to the hatch. Promise you won't run?

'We'll be the first out, Mum. First in, first out. Good eh?' Let's make light of so ridiculous a disaster. Let's not build fallout shelters in earnest; let's just ridicule it, so no-one thinks the holocaust is feasible.

No, she says, I want to stay and die.

'You're not going to die. I won't let you.' I love thus to cast myself as wicked protectress, as frustrator of hopes, as Bad Angel.

People read on planes. Most people. When there is no movie. On Air Canada, there is no movie.

My mother cannot read. She is literate, you understand, but cannot read. I had not expected this. When I last saw her, she could still read. I never dreamt that my letters to her were read out by a nurse. I would have written them differently.

'Why? What's happened?'

She explains, with difficulty, for she is tired and thirsty, that her eyes can no longer scan the lines, no longer move correctly to read consecutively. I am stunned. Surely this would be left her till the end, I had thought? So all the magazines go back into the flight bag. I cannot very well sit here reading if she is unable to. Many things have I done while she looked on from wheelchair, car, even sleigh: horse riding, ice skating, swimming. But there is no spectator value in reading.

'I'll get you a drink. We'll be the last, being at the

24

back.' I go up to the trolley, miles down towards the middle section of the plane.

'We'll get to you in due course. Please be patient. I can't let you walk down with drinks. Inshirrance.'

Inshirrance has a lot to answer for. I find a conical paper cup in the toilet and fill it with Eau Potable. She tilts her head back and I try to remember how to give her a drink. Most of it goes down her neck and onto her turquoise blouse; the rest chokes her.

'How do you usually drink nowadays, Mum?'

'Pee-u-pett' she says. That's what she *says*.

'What do you mean, exactly?'

'Pee-u-pett' she gasps, angry to be asked to repeat a word for me. I rack the brains. She will never, never substitute a word for the one she has said; it is a mental block. She repeats and repeats things until she is apoplectic and the listener develops a similar mental block, one in which the only word in the world is the one being heard and it has no meaning. Repeat a word like 'pity' twenty times and see what happens. Now what does it mean? Nothing. It sounds ridiculous, like something you call a cat with: here pitypitypitypitypity!

Puppet. What puppet can you drink through? A child's joke without a punchline. Think laterally, it's the only hope. Pipette: a feeding straw for premature babies.

'A straw!' She never shares the triumph of the listener's vanquishing of the mental block; it is the least you can do, being sound and healthy. She ignores me and I order a small bottle of ginger ale for her, with a straw.

She sucks it magnificently well, efficiently. I congratulate her. She smiles, like a child praised. See, I have learnt to drink from a straw. I must have smiled like that when first weaned from the bottle, up at her. Did I? Did she? I feel dizzy and confused myself which could be the result of the 'free' white wine I have been given, without a straw.

'We still have the toilet to do.'

She asks me if I will have a cigarette for her. *For* her? I have got some, for emergencies. It seems she can't smoke any more but can enjoy it second-hand. The nurses came and smoked in her face for her at the nursing home. What a picture it conjures: groups of nurses locking her door from the inside, perhaps one on sentry duty in case Matron should catch them, sitting around the bed smoking at her beatific face, and later opening the window to clear away the smell. Conspiracy. She must have enjoyed that.

The steward thinks it best if he simply carries her to the toilet, but she won't have it, for obvious reasons. I eye up the passengers for a beefy woman to help me, for the pants have to be down before she hits the seat. I chicken out, for equally obvious reasons. It is too much to ask. The stewardess who had been walloped is nowhere to be seen during these negotiations. I could lift her, though not for long, but I could not do the pants at the same time.

Finally the copy-stewardess arrives from the First Class, announces that she is a Trained Nurse and has Seen Worse. She takes off her jacket, rolls up her sleeves and blows at her fringe, which she would call 'bangs', as if we are about to shift a piano to the upstairs.

My mother insists on telling the Trained One that she too is a Trained Nurse. When I have translated it between cries of pain engendered by banging my hip everywhere, the stewardess is puzzled, as if a black man in a loincloth had told her he has a degree from Oxford. It could be true, but is irrelevant. Not to my mother: it is her sole paper qualification and represents the happiest times of her life.

How she puts up with the degradation of it, of being 'potted' like a toddler, congratulated by the Trained One and myself, for producing so quickly, with both of us, all three of us, crammed into the toilet which measures about eighteen inches square, for we found that we could not both leave without removing her support.

'Some people just can't go with an audience' says the

Trained One, and I take to her instantly, for she concentrates well and we have the pants in a trice.

'I'm afraid my mother never has the opportunity to do otherwise.'

As we struggle back with her, fireman's-chair fashion, the stewardess's mouth comes close to my ear and she whispers something to me.

'Cancer, is it?'

'No, what?' She has to go: someone is buzzing her down the aisle.

We sit, not reading.

'Perhaps you should sleep now.' I fear she might tell me that for some reason she can no longer sleep; no longer dream, no longer rest at all. Even sleep, perhaps, is an activity requiring aim or co-ordination. I tilt the chair back and wedge her in with blankets from the Trained One. We tuck and tuck, to prevent her lurching forward in unconsciousness. It is like the primitive swaddling of an infant, a severely malnourished infant, whose flesh can no longer support its bones, no longer warm them, protect them, direct them. I saw a film of black people starving, on a dusty floor, in family groups, and a mother made a tender gesture towards a small black bundle of dying child: she whisked a fly away in slow motion. It was not sentimental. It was an expression of futility, of hopelessness. The world is coming to an end: let us brush away the flies. What else is there useful to do?

Let us tuck and tuck and swaddle the collection of molecules, the disordered arrangement, which was once my mother.

Sing me a song, she says, a lullaby.

'I can't do that. People will think I'm mad.'

Who cares, she says, what people think?

I started to sing, softly, without conviction.

> Golden slumbers kiss your eyes
> Smiles awake you when you rise

Sleep pretty da-a-arling
Do-o not cry, and I
Will sing
A lull-
A-bye.

Nobody minds my singing after all – but public reaction to her noises which begin as sleep overtakes her, is hostile. The 'noises' are like the moaning of a woman in labour – rhythmic, rising to a crescendo and falling to a low wail. It is only the phase of shallow sleep, and will pass, but while it lasts, people come up to ask me to put a stop to it. One woman tells me it is frightening her child to death; the child is shaking and sobbing.

'Tell your child it is a sick mermaid in the hold,' I reply. 'Use your imagination. This is a very sick person who needs to sleep, and it won't last long.'

But it seems to be lasting indefinitely, like she will. I want to tell them all, via the public address system, that she has suffered more in one day than they will in the whole of their lucky lives.

The Trained One comes and stands, looking and listening, without hostility. She is, I decide, what you might call a Brick. May I call you a Brick? May I give you a medal? May I burst into tears on the padded maroon of your jacket?

'She looks peaceful. I'll try to get the pilot to say things over the intercom to cover the noise.'

She means it.

He tells us about the atmospheric conditions, about flight paths, about the size and capacity of the engine, each engine in turn, then about where he trained, and for how long; how he had been in 'Nam for a while, flying helicopters. The passengers are hooked – magazines are being laid down, books put away, as the pilot drones on about offensives without adequate food or fuel or equipment, when he and his pal were in enemy lines for two days without sleep . . . But the noises come to an end finally and my mother is asleep, and the Trained One

28

goes to tell the pilot to wind it up now. Suddenly he says:

'Have a nice day now' and clicks off.

There are murmurings of disappointment in the aisles. People are muttering, 'tantalising' and 'should finish what you start', but gradually it dies down.

The relief.

She can still sleep.

My body slackens. I will try to sleep too. But I am the one who has lost this knack of drifting off to sleep. It is not the fact that my knees are touching the seat in front, or my head is not quite at the right height for the head-rest, or my arms are without anywhere to be. I have slept in worse places: on the gearboxes of lorries, on wooden benches on ferries during gales on the Channel, on cold marble floors, in small cars crowded with people. It is her presence next to me, and the thousands of miles between me and the Atlantic Ocean beneath. Not yet the true Atlantic for we are still in Canada technically, over Newfoundland by now: a little-known place about the size of Europe.

Opening my eyes makes it worse. She's still there. What is it that is so frightening about the features of a relative suffering, dying? The similarity perhaps: the fact that your own features, however much you deny it, are carried there, distorted there. Of course, tempered by another. So that I may think my forehead is not that wide, or that shiny or that white, that my eyebrows are not that dark, nor my hair, and not so fierce and do not meet in the middle, but it does me no good. For there is the nose, no denying it. My eyeballs may be smaller, or set differently, or perhaps her eyes only bulged recently with loss of weight?

Her eyes were always the killers. Stone dead with a look. You felt absolutely certain, in the glare of those orbs, that you were guilty of the sins of the entire world and then some. Once, in the African uplight before the six o'clock rains, I saw in her eyes veins, cones, rods; saw them quite differently as organs, just organs. It was a revelation. I had imagined doing an ocularectomy: there, Gloucester, better off without them, troublesome organs.

They are shut now, of course. But the eyelids seem under strain, as if being shut were unnatural; they might at any moment open under pressure.

There are hundreds of normal people here. Able-bodied. Only they don't know it. They don't think of themselves as able-bodied. They are not Registered Able-Bodied for the purposes of Income Tax.

Sleep, cease packing your bags, you are going nowhere.

The Norms are making delicate movements they take for granted: turning the pages of a book, lighting a cigarette with a single flame the first time, scanning pictures and words accurately with their eyeballs, lifting drinks off the table-flap without looking up from the page, knowing where the hand is going to without having to look. The veritable Kings and Queens of the Earth, but they do not realize. They are bored, restless, and dissatisfied. Wake up, all you Norms, from your ungolden slumbers.

Sleep, wait, where are you off to?

The tight eyeballs are flickering with rapid eye movement now. What could she be dreaming of? Does she walk in her dreams, talk in her dreams? Or have her disabilities caught up with her? Sometimes the house you moved away from is still the set for dreams years later. Sometimes not. Traumas go straight into dream, without preamble. Her life is one major trauma, and would need no lapse of time. The subconscious would greet the facts of her condition as an old friend: oh, yes, I know it well, that one where you run and never move, and your body won't obey you: a very common nightmare down here, so what's new? Your eyes follow a line of words but you can't decipher the meaning? Old hat. Can't seem to make people understand you when you speak? Yes, that old chestnut.

Sleep, for once, have pity on me.

Why do I feel so uneasy? Everything is going well, is fine. For you have to judge these things relatively. Except that memories will keep ambushing me, trapped here in this uncomfortable place, as if I am about to do something unmentionable, something irrevocable. As if it is her or me, as it has always seemed to be.

Sleep, aren't we old friends?

In the past. Surely we saw it coming, knew it before it was upon her? Didn't her walk become detached from the floor years and years ago? Feet floating for one instant to the next as if there were no continuous trust to be put in the laws of gravity? Wasn't there disconnection there, later between one word and another?

'Will passengers kindly fasten their seat belts as we are experiencing a little turbulence as we descend towards Gander. *Mesdames et messieurs* . . .'

Each turbulent gesture overstepped the mark, each feeling outgrew its object, temper volcanic, love oceanic.

All the parts grotesquely out of proportion, like panic in an eggshell?

'Extinguish all cigarettes, remove objects from your lap.'

Removal. Always, yes. She even removed our childhoods; they were no longer appropriate and did not suit her needs. Come with me to the Bush, Janey. Dust-yellow is the colour and texture of panic to this day. Took me to show me driving 'just in case anything happens when we are alone out in the car': boasting of being the youngest driver in the world, why didn't I sense impending tragedy? Oh, why didn't I cry, when I laughed? Crashing gear upon gear through my cruel adolescence, her calm then shattered, for catastrophe was befriending her against her will.

'We will be landing shortly in Newfoundland. Passengers will vacate the aeroplane while refuelling and maintenance checks take place. Kindly take all hand baggage with you.'

Alright, Walloped One, the joke has gone far enough: I will leave this plane at Heathrow and not before.

The front of the plane is tipping down, the aisle falling away. I have fastened my belt and am holding the armrest on the other side of my mother, to trap her in.

We could be 'crashing shortly at Gander'. They wouldn't tell us, would they? Why tell them? Better not knowing, for what you don't know, can't . . . the ground is approaching so fast, it might as well be the end of the world. I'm glad my mother is asleep, this time.

At first, I did think that. She is so ill, she will simply go in her sleep. One morning, she'll be dead.

But morning after morning came and she was not dead, just living and angry about it. We saw, my brother and I, but did not register: banging our shoulders, then waists, then hips, against handrails not there the day before. Bravado was the order of the day: 'You'll get better, bound to. See if you don't.' And smiled and smiled.

Smiling, as her words were beaten senseless by her tongue before we heard them: she couldn't speak our language any more and with the loss of words came losses so enormous not one of us could name it. She could no longer let go of anything – objects held on to her; she could not shift her gaze minutely or in time with thoughts. Images held on to her and strangled her; bunched, drastic, ungainly, sudden, tense: a daemon strength in faery movements. Fluttering, waving, stiff, brittle arms grasped and overshot a million times a day. Fingernails dug loving-deep into familiar flesh, tears in our unprotesting eyes proof of a painful attachment. Love? Or was maternal feeling gone too in the passing casual violence of her every gesture? The foundations of the physical world were gone; she wanted us to anchor her somewhere, with touch, with kisses, and with speech. But we withdrew, as you do, from disaster, from Catastrophe. Like astronauts in space, she was bereft of stimuli and her mind came adrift.

The first bump of the runway throws her against my arm and I ease her back towards the chair. It's only Newfoundland, Mum, not Heaven.

So, if we knew it, foresaw it, kept mum about it, never screamed, raged, ran amok, it was a testament to human endurance. Or was it cowardice? One by one, we left. But there is no absolute leaving: there is something of her in us still, and something of us in her. The geography changes – volcanic, flooded, arid, impassable – but not the suffering. It only intensifies. It does not diminish because we are no longer there to witness it. I am here now, back at the beginning of time; I have made no progress. I sit next to her on the dark plain, shot through with her misery, the spores of her within me, and I know that there will be no dawn here: it can only get darker and darker.

I gather to me the drugs, any ten of which could probably send her home for good. Oh, give me the strength to do it. Give me the strength.

'You had better stay on board with her,' says the Trained One.

'You're a Brick.'

'What?'

'An English expression: you're okay.'

If Canada were simply a motorway, Gander would be that petrol station which could have the sign 'Last Chance to buy Fuel before the Atlantic' in the forecourt. Most traffic flying from Canada to the rest of the world, eastwards, stops here for a quick gulp, and since the traffic is so predictable and so constant, Newfoundland makes almost no provision for the many human beings who are forced to spend an unwanted half an hour within the walls of Gander Airport. It is a relief indeed to be allowed the privilege of not having to sit in Gander Airport: worth paying for.

4   Paradoxy

Have any of you ever sat alone, but for the unconscious invalid, on an empty plane, near the back, with silence but for the sluicing sound of millions of gallons of highly flammable aeroplane fuel being poured into a tank beneath you? Has anyone, in the History of Man, been so tempted to light a match, chuck it out of the now open hatch behind, and put an end to it all?

I simply sit here, between my sleeping mother and the porthole, clutching the packets of sedatives, stimulants, and contraceptives. Waiting.

If we had been already in England, the woman who comes in to empty the ashtrays would be saying 'You didn't ought to be 'ere; oh, I see; what a crying shame' but since it is still Canada, she says 'Have a nice day' and minds her own business, carrying on down the aisles.

Presently, when she is gone, I squeeze out from my seat and investigate the First Aid box by the galley and steal a small bottle of white wine from the tiny fridge nearby.

The First Aid box is surprisingly chaotic, considering the regimentation of the 'kitchen'. There are leaflets on in-flight heart attacks, in-flight childbirth, in-flight death. The pilot's decision is final in all cases. Typical: he never has to turn in-flight midwife, does he? There is a pamphlet on coping with nuclear attack. I hadn't thought of that. Suppose the Bomb goes off, down, whatever, while we are *up here*! Someone will be in an aeroplane if/when it does. It might be this plane, why not?

How do we get down? And why bother? There is a map with 'friendly zones' listed. It is probably best not to inform the passengers of the exact nature and extent of the attack, in order to 'minimize panic'. Ah, yes. This is just to announce that Nuclear War has broken out, but we are happy to say it is only minor, only slightly awful, and eternal nuclear winter is many many days away. So, strap yourselves in, light up a few fags, drink yourself silly until we land in Northern Greenland, where the people will greet us with unparalleled friendliness, emerging from their nuclear fallout shelters just to see to us, feed us, shake hands with us.

They will only be armed to protect us from bears.

Tired little teddy-bears, with two heads.

I sip my wine, and wait, in the rising heat of the non-air-conditioning.

It's alright; it won't happen. Not here. Not to us.

Not to me.

Especially not to me.

I am double-entered on the world; I will have to die twice. This is because I have two passports, which is how I manage to leave one country on Friday night, enter another on Saturday morning, leave that one on Sunday evening and enter the first one again on Monday morning, all without leaving trace anywhere of having emigrated; no trace, even for the CIA to follow. Not that they would want to.

They should, though. I am subversion itself. I wasn't properly brought up. More important things were going on. The anarchy is not a form of words, not just a joke; it is bone-marrow deep. There is no less comforting thought than that you are simply the result of centuries of random accidents, one of which made you a gambler at birth, a coin in mid-toss.

And while my mother, and all those later destined to join her at Lourdes, should she survive to go there, turn in their spastic, flailing way towards a Loving God (see how He loves you to pieces), I turn towards the Majesty of the Random, a wicked God, in tune with the modern world.

'You, J Wells, have dual citizenship, but your mother, Mrs C Wells, does not?' says the customs official who has climbed on board to question me.

'A conundrum, isn't it? I was born in two places at once.'

'Could you explain to me this puzzle?' He is about thirteen and still has those enormous ears which will shrink later.

'Physically, I was born in England, but the Canadians see this as an accident. Spiritually, I was born in Canada, but abroad.'

'Ah, you have a Born-Abroad Certificate?' Can you believe that there is such a thing? No wonder I can never be Born Again. The light is dawning on Big-Ears. I show him my bilingual documents stating the Born Abroadness. He is well pleased.

'I was born in Calcutta,' he confides. I was going to say, that accounts for your being so black, but some people are sensitive about that.

'Physically or spiritually?'

The passengers, looking very much the worse for their 'rest' at the god-forsaken worst airport in the world, clamber on, sweating with the heat and smelling of melting pine sap.

They are all congratulating the one man who managed to buy a beer. He is attempting, even now, to share it out. I have been drinking cold wine and feel much refreshed. We might make it over the Drink after all. A certain cameraderie is emerging now among the Patients, and we have not had to crash or be hijacked. Shall we conclude from this that a little suffering has ennobled their Souls? Rash, a little rash, I think. Besides, the notion is crap.

There are even more trees at Gander than at Halifax. Not interesting trees; repetitive evergreen trees. No competition: a branches-down win for Newfoundland. Man has not ignored, nor ear seen, nor mouth smelled, etc, the enormity of the Newfie Forest. And where the

36

forest balds for a moment, pyran ʼds of nut-brown trunks fill the space. As we take off, my arm braced against my mother, the whole island is laid out like a green map, or a plaster mould made by a meticulous boy for a train to pass by. However, I don't believe they have yet invented the train there.

A smell of hot tin foil pervades the cooling air as we level off. Dinner is coming. I will have to wake her. As soon as she tries to open her eyes, I can see something is wrong. First of all, she can't.

They are stuck together. Oh, Unmerciful One, why heap everything on her; why not share it out, like the beer can there, and let everyone in the plane have one of her complaints? What is this new thing?

This time there is no need to bother the staff; I go straight to the already-researched First Aid cupboard myself to find cotton wool and a sachet of distilled water. Bathing opens them, but they are dreadful: red, bloodshot and oozing pus.

'How long have you had this, Mum?' Ages and ages, she says, but don't worry, just get the trays down for dinner, she's starving. I'm not having this, so I find the male Steward, whom I have not yet offended, the Trained One being busy with dinners, and ask him whether he thinks he has any chloremycetin on board.

'You asking me! Airport Security told me you have every drug known to man in your hand luggage.'

'Everything but what I need, isn't it always the way? Even Optrex might help. Could you look please?'

He finds a whole museum of sticking plaster: from tins with gummy cloth the colour of no flesh (neither black nor white, but orangey-brown) to the present-day invisible aerated sellotape Band-Aids, but no eyedrops of any sort. He consults the passenger list and finds three doctors. One is an archaeologist, one a man in a dog-collar, and one has a black bag discreetly between his feet, from which he donates a sachet of brine and a dropper. A Man of Stone, a Man of the Cloth, and the Giver of Salt.

Meanwhile the Trained One is cutting up my mother's food for her. I can't believe it. Sometimes a small kindness makes you want to cry. The big kindnesses just fill you with awe, and respect, but the little ones shatter you. My mother is smiling and seems to be communicating with her. Approaching, I realize that the Trained One is laughing and nodding imaginatively, *as if* she understood, and mother is fooled. I can never fool her, of course. She assumes that I am not interested in anything she might have to say, out of sheer malice, and so not bothering to understand.

It doesn't make any sense, does it, not *bothering* to understand? How can you, could you, do it? Unless you are trying to cover up the murder you are being questioned about: 'Kill her, what do you *mean*?' That's obvious, but otherwise? The door to understanding is never ajar, surely, it is either shut or open?

But the Trained One, cutting up your food, has a licence. It is the 'no need' of it which chokes me too. What she understands, somehow, is that to seem to have trouble in understanding will offend.

'Thank you. Thank you.' I keep saying, like an idiot, trying to get drops into the bloodshot eyes from behind. It is a well-known fact that the inside of an aeroplane is designed with able-bodied dwarves in mind. I can think of no way to get back to my seat now that my mother's tray with the dissected meal on it is filling the tiny gap between her knees and the back of the seat in front. I will have to climb over the back of my seat, behind which there is only the gap for the escape-hatch and then the toilets. Good thing I wore the jeans, Aunty.

The Steward is hanging around, watching. Does he find my predicament amusing? People don't have predicaments in aeroplanes, do they? They just conform, behave themselves, exhibit patience, get a bit tipsy or totally drunk, and fall asleep.

'Give me a leg up, then.' The Steward grins the all-Canadian grin, with teeth.

'You gonna *climb*?'

'Do I have any choice?'

He giggles, and seems to double up behind the seat. Actually he is cupping his two hands together for me to step into. He might catapult me several seats along, out of mischievousness, or malice. No. If I break my neck, they will have to find the leaflet on in-flight traction, and would be stuck with my mother's demands for hours. I am safe, as usual.

As my weight shifts forwards, as I become self-sufficient so to speak, there is no need for the extra support, for the hands around the waist, for the shove from behind. Perhaps he is trying to be helpful. Or provocative? Or teasing?

It is a timely reminder, as I crumple for impact, that I am still a person, female. Nearly forgot again. Nearly regressed into something else.

My mother wants to know where I have been all this time.

'Behind the seat, climbing back.'

No, before that.

'I had to wash my hands, after doing your eyes. It's very contagious.'

What is very contagious, she wants to know.

'Conjunctivitis.'

That's what I think she's got, is it? And since when am I an authority on it? When did I train to be a doctor?

'Let's eat, shall we?' It is a good thing I never did train to be a doctor, for, in her eyes, I would then have joined the legion of the Quacks, the hordes of totally despicable distorters of the Truth. For only my own mother knows the Truth, Absolute and Indisputable, about Matters Medical; doctors simply pretend. Didn't she, herself, with her own eyes, see too many botched operations, misdiagnoses, downright skulduggery, ever to have confidence in the medical profession again? In a way, she has a right to despise the members of a profession which deals out health and the promise of cure to the entire world, except her. A justifiable paranoia, I always thought.

I only ever think of myself, she is saying, not enough of other people. It is a great failing in me. If only I would show some sympathy for her, it would be the better. Did I think I was the only person in the world that *mattered*? Ridiculous.

She is right, of course. Though I dabbed at her eyes efficiently, though I left no corner unwashed, no part of the tensile surface untreated with saline, there was no tenderness in it. No sympathy. Just calm, and a scientific thoroughness. This is how I have to approach her. I cannot dare to let myself sympathize. It would be madness to invite intimacy. Especially the eyes, the explicit screening of her suffering.

How she aimed the first morsel to her mouth, I will never know, but she cannot manage the second.

'That spoon's a wash-out. Use your hands. Who cares what people think, eh?' She manages a small piece of steak and is still chewing it when I have finished my entire meal.

Now I have learnt to bolt my food, it's true. I am the first to finish at dinner parties, to the consternation of hostesses who say, worried, 'Have you had enough?', or rudely, 'How *do* you keep your figure?' However, even I never finished a whole meal before someone's second mouthful. At this rate she will be starting her dessert at Heathrow.

'I've finished. Shall I help you?' There, thinking of others, just as she suggested. Others being her, of course.

How do I propose to assist her in chewing her food, she would like to know?

'I mean, I could spoon it in for you.

But the problem isn't getting it into the mouth, she informs me, her anger rising, but chewing and swallowing once it is there. It seems this whole event is the result of my stupidity, my malice, my selfishness.

Ah, what adage could the goodly Gloria coin for this? A choking man will clutch at a straw? A fool and his food are soon parted? A hungry woman is an angry one? That's the one. One swallow does not a dinner make . . .

40

'It's always like this, is it?'

Did I think she was putting it on for my amusement? No, it isn't all that funny, not really. But maybe later, for even disability has to be laughed at, in order to be survived, I might tell the enormous Irish woman next door we mostly chewed the cud, a lot of jawing, me and me Mam, you know, gnashing our teeth: pulverising the past into bite-sized pieces; the whole flight was one long lunch really, I might say.

'Oh boy,' says the Steward, 'have we got a sewing machine or a tumble-drier, is it? Want the window open a little for some fresh air?' I grin, without teeth. A man who gropes thighs surreptitiously is in no position to refuse the request of a passenger. 'Food not to your liking?' he continues, looking down at my mother's uneaten meal.

'This is a challenge for you guys,' I begin, in my best Nova Scotian, as soon as the Walloped One has swanned off into the First Class, ignoring me.

'Let me guess.'

'What we need is a blender. Liquidizer?' Which is the Canadian, which the English? Hard to know with transatlantic imports: they had them first, so we may have adopted their word. 'What do you call it, that mashes things into a pulp?'

'Bulldozer?'

'You're not trying. What do you call it?'

'Impossible, whatever it is.'

'No-one's ever asked for a purée?'

'Babies' he says, to the Trained One, coming in with an empty trolley.

'Wotchya need to know about babies?' she asks him, winking rather oddly. She sets down cloths and lists, takes the plate-tray from me, empties it and washes the little compartments under a tap. Then she opens four tins of Heinz Baby Food Stage One, two savoury and two 'dessert' (in England they print 'pudding'). She spoons them carefully into appropriate sections.

41

'Don't tell her what it is,' she advises, having warmed it briefly and added salt and sugar. The food seems to vary only in what shade of brown it is.

I won't have to tell her what it is, will I? She will know, won't she? She being a one-time health visitor, black bag full of baby-food samples? But did she ever taste her wares?

It is the best and fastest meal she has eaten for years, she says. Her compliments to the chef. Well done, Heinz. I compose a letter to them in my head, advising them to branch out into Disabled Person's Food. Only the labels need to be different, and they may buy the idea from me at a reasonable cost.

The sad truth is that my mother is becoming a baby. No, worse. She has already done so. Only the mind won't fit: it is the mind of a fifty-year-old woman who has had two children, one of whom is here to torment or assist her, depending on how you view it.

Everything is relative.

I light a cigarette and smoke it for her.

'There's a fag by proxy,' I say, squeezing her all-bone knee; like the knee of a wooden chair whose upholstery has mostly gone, it offers unexpected resistance.

'Doxy!' she says, perfectly. It shocks me that she says it so perfectly, not that I am once again going to have to hear from her that it means 'prostitute' and appears in a poem by . . . The magic of Heinz: for do not chronological babies start to speak once they eat solids?

She recites now, with infinite slowness and terrible distortion, so that even I can only understand one word in five, looking as it were through the smoked glass of the door of understanding without being able to open it; only the desolation, the seediness of that sick Pre-Raphaelite poetry seeps through, under the door. Her recitation may be something like this:

For . winter's . rains . and . ruins . seasons . of . snows . and . sins . light . loses . night . wins . it . is . enough . the . end . and . the . beginning . are . one . thing . night . long . within . mine . arms . I . have . been . faithful . to . thee . Doxy . in . my . fashion.

Or not.

Still, I know what she means; that's the trouble, I *know*. I cannot deny this association through words, this love of sounds. She was amazed once at the daring of the 'bee-loud' glade – how could anyone think of saying it, dare to say it? I too shuddered with 'Ah! Bright wings.' and wondered how anyone could have thought of saying *that*.

Where are our bright wings now, mother? If they are still there, dimly visible behind the smoked glass, they seem to be twitching in the last floored spasm of dying.

It is important. It is our only common ground; so she blows it. She always blows it.

Because she is dribbling now with the naughtiness of *that* word, not the rightness, the richness of the others, and I have to wipe now her saliva'd pleasure from the napkin-bib on her chest, ignoring the wicked glint in her gummy eyes, and pretend, for the hundredth time, not to know that a Doxy is a 'prozshdeetude' as she tells me. But I cannot ignore her stiffening, withdrawing from my attentions to say, all too clearly, that she regards my father's new wife as . . . and the hate is there, and the anger, not distorted, just magnified in the Midas eyes. Even though it is not my fault, it cannot ever be my fault, any of that, the eyes are still beaming the hate and anger *directly at me*. And I pretend to myself that I couldn't possibly compromise a little with a poor, dying, crippled person, and agree with her, say, 'yes, awful, isn't it', just this once.

Which is why, of course, it *is* my bloody fault, all of it, because silence is assent. I am agreeing to it.

'Stop it. I don't talk about that. We agreed.'

* * *

The sky outside is dark now. Just a brief night which we will soon pass through, for we fly into the sunlight, chasing the 'busie old foole', and awaiting the miraculous sight ofa new dawn we don't yet deserve to see.

My mother is saying that I must not say hurtful things to her because she will not last long, how can she in her condition, and so anything I say to her might be the last thing anyone said to her on earth. She might take it with her to the grave. Did I want that?

'Then you want only lies and half-truths, do you?'

Is the truth always so terrible? she wants to know. Have I nothing good to tell her?

There is a faint streak of a hint of light appearing now around one side of my porthole. A promise of grey.

'I have got something to tell you.'

She waits. Does she know? Are such people as her (what people? – there are none) gifted with pre-knowledge: is half-life clairvoyant?

'I'm married.' Yes, she did know, though she says nothing.

There, if that is the last thing she ever hears, it should set her mind at rest on two counts: I am not unmarriageable, not a lesbian. She widens her eyes, her black brows shoot up and she gapes open her mouth. She is overdoing it. A grotesquery of Surprise: a mask from some ancient Japanese play, white wood and black paint.

'Just recently. We eloped. You know Christopher.'

There, I have compromised for her. A little powdery white cosmetic half-truth to sniff at and nod over. For I know she knows that we did not elope, that we had a quiet register office wedding, to which my father, of whom we do not speak, came and was witness. And she may even have guessed that his new wife came also.

There is a pause. The universe outside slackens, spreads a little. The grey seeps from around the corner to just visible. I continue to look out of the window. People are putting their arms into the air as if to ask the teacher whether they may go to the toilet, and switching

44

off their lights, directing their air-conditioning away from their eyes to sleep. The Trained One is handing out blankets, turning off the overhead lights, settling them all down to sleep, her whispering aisles of babes, as she goes. I turn, finally, to see whether she is still there, still alive, so quiet has the whole world gone.

Tears are running out of her sore eyes and the pus sparkles green in the corners.

'Mummy! What is it?'

'Doooooyoooooluvmeeeee?' she wails. The Trained One is standing over us now, with blankets, offering. I wave them away. We have hundreds. We can't move for them, we are smothered.

'Of course I do,' I say too slowly, too late. And if I had meant it, I would never have said it. I would have scooped up my poor little bundle of a Mummy and squeezed her to death.

I look out of the window again, and will not touch her, or mean it. Not just now. I wanted congratulations. I wanted a conventional mother for a moment, like I had done on the morning of the wedding itself. Only twice in my life: then and now. Failed, failed, failed. Not that I have any right. A conventional, loving daughter would have moved Heaven and Earth to allow her crippled mother to sit in on the ceremony. We have failed each other. Let us leave it there.

The Trained One will not leave us alone. She comes back and hands me a bowl of water with cotton-wool balls floating in it. I can't think what it is for a moment, and then sponge the eyes and hand it back.

You are so kind, my mother tries to say.

'Yer welcome' replies the Trained One, as if she has understood.

'Shall we sleep now?' How come you still have the power to terrify, Mummy? How come you are such a presence still in your tiny turquoise suit, now splattered with substances, your hair in the air like a neglected privet? Dominance is still, paradoxically, yours.

No, she has already slept, *thank* you very much.

45

5 Northern Lights

Seven hours, six with a tail wind, isn't bad really, considering the distance between the continents of North America and Europe. When you think that it can take you an hour and a half to get from Ealing to Lewisham, it's not bad. Almost pleasant really, if you can spend the time reading, sleeping, eating, drinking, even watching movies. Even if none of these activities are available, that much silence and solitude is alright, is bearable.

But there are four hours to go at least, no sign of a tail wind, and the greyness I thought I saw, on the horizon I thought I had seen, is growing so imperceptibly that there is not yet any promise of real dawn.

Four hours to go, and Mummy and I have fallen out.

The night is dark and long and emptier up here than anywhere else. If the world tilted on its axis suddenly, like the head of a coquettish girl, to one side, we could spin off into space. Life *is* that fragile up here, that random. So, let us rejoice!

'Have you such a thing as a rosary on you, Mummy?'

Blessed by the Bishop of Halifax, she replies, but I am not to see it, not to touch it, for I am an Unbeliever. Would I sap some of its blessedness from it, simply by looking with atheist eyes?

'I thought we could say a few hundred Hail Marys, to pass the time. Spiritual credit in the Heavenly Bank?'

Apparently, her account is quite in order in that respect. She is excused, she says, from any such observances on account of her handicaps. Intercession has been paid for and is made on her behalf by other people. She can die at any time, and need not have the Last Rites, unless there is opportunity.

How reassuring. I begin to lose the thread of what she is saying when she speaks for any length of time, and the meal seems to have given her strength, for she speaks and speaks.

What she prays for, it seems, is for the hand of God to intercede and take her. She prays for death to come soon. Surely she is not capable of committing any sins now (other than those of the mind, which are only secondary after all) due to her physical condition, which is almost like that of God's Innocents – the babes. Here I have to nod in agreement. It is the wisest thing she has said for hours.

So why, she wonders continually (and who wouldn't) does He not take her, now that she is ready? It has occurred to her that an agent will present himself, or herself, someone who can deliver her with impunity. Someone who could do God's work, without a bad conscience. A minister, or a medical person. To this end, it is stipulated on the medical records which I carry with me, that she is to be given no antibiotics, or transfusions, or any drugs, means or devices designed to prevent an infection or disease from terminating her life, for if it be God's will so to take her, His Will Be Done.

Will this document be binding on another doctor?

'But you might die a horrible lingering sort of death, in pain!' The calmness of the contemplation here must be a test of some sort; you don't flirt with your own demise like this.

Or, she says, looking straight at me for the first time since I announced my change in marital status, she could die suddenly, with the help of someone who did not believe in God, who did not fear retribution. For if there is no God, mortal sin becomes a charitable act. They even have a legal word for it: Euthanasia.

Someone, she says, looking straight at me, at her own daughter, someone with a big heart, full of mercy.

'Mummy, what are you saying?'

You have all the drugs, she says, you have them there. I'll tell you what to do. Wait until I am back in England: I want to die there. In the nursing home, settled in.

I cannot stop the tears; neither do I know why I am crying, not exactly.

No, no, she says, do it now, it's best. We'll end it here. Don't you think it is about bloody time? And you can bury me in England. Cremate I mean. It makes no difference. I don't want to draw it out: that would be bad for you. You can say I took the pills by accident. It could happen. You could phone my priest in Canada and he would hear your Confession and absolve you.

Absolve me?

'No, no, no.'

I can't *manage*, she says, I need assistance in everything. Don't you think I would have seen to it myself otherwise? You know I would have. Help me. Just this once. I'll never need anything again.

She was gasping now, hardly making intelligible words.

Ever. Again. Just. Help. I. Jane!

'I'm free now, if anyone should want a little visit to the ladies' room,' says the Trained One, suddenly there, over us, in charge. I jump up. My mother is smiling, nodding, happy. She thinks she has persuaded me. She reads my mind. She has been doing it since 1952. I stagger and climb out to assist in the little trip to the ladies' room.

The plane has become a nightmare place, too small to run away in, too dark to see where you are going. The Steward is silently standing by with a torch. This is not a campsite; why does he have a torch?

'The lights are out in the washrooms,' he says.

The plane is simply a forgotten tube of flimsy metal hurtling through the night sky over the Atlantic with a random assortment of people fumbling about in the dark. Nobody knows we are here. Nobody cares. Underneath us is a world so sophisticated it is disappearing up its own backside: a world where my mother ought to have faded by some ditchside, crumpled, uncared for – where by now her suffering would have been well over. I want it to be over, over.

'Over! Over! Come on!' The Trained One is gasping at me as we shift the little bundle of flesh in and out of the torch beam over the bowl of the toilet. There is the sound of raindrops hitting a corrugated tin roof, as the urine reaches the dry metal disc beneath. I used to think the wee was sucked out onto the world, warning those below with a little red light that it was coming.

Over the planet.

Over the brink of the world-bowl, the Drink, the Atlantic swelling indifferently beneath our tube.

Oh God, how could you leave us on this dark and dying planet with no torch?

I am weeping into the darkness as we inch back to our seats with the body.

Then I go myself in the pitchy black and wait for the dawn to break. I try to think of nothing, of blackness. I watch the blackness through the window for inspiration, but it betrays me by breaking up to reveal patches of green, blue, yellow, orange. Is this what dawn looks like from above?

I had thought of ending it *for* her, but not in *collusion* with her; that is different.

The door beside me opens and a beam of light falls in. It is not the Holy Ghost, merely the Steward.

'Bloody Hell, I might have been *using* the toilet.'

'I knew you weren't. Just having a break, aren't you?'

He uncaps a miniature and hands it to me, still standing in the narrow doorway with the torch under his arm like a rifle. 'I don't blame you at all.' We are whispering, because people do in the dark, unless they are being attacked.

Besides, raised voices would reach my mother.

'Look at this sunrise!' I say, for something to say.

He laughs, nearly dropping the torch-rifle.

49

'That's not the sunrise.'

'What is it, then?'

'The Northern Lights. The pilot wanted to wake every-one up to show them, but we dissuaded him.'

'Why? He ought to.'

'He's said enough this flight, what with his "flights" of fancy earlier.'

'Never in Vietnam?'

'Never anyplace but here.'

'He is a *good* pilot, though, isn't he?'

'Yes, shirr. Just a bit pissed at the moment, so the Co is taking us.'

'Listen, I'm a passenger. You're supposed to reassure me.'

'I don't think of you as a passenger any more. We've been through too much together.'

I've crossed the dividing line, somehow, have I? It makes me feel insecure, as if I had, like the steward-esses, some superstitious responsibility for the other passengers, and the safety of the crossing. I take a swig at the, what is it, vodka?

'You married?' he asks. It seems so irrelevant, here in the dark, now.

'Yes,' I say, 'just very recently. Are you?' Only the second person I have ever told.

'No. I'm gay.' I must have been imagining the thigh-stroke. Neither is the sunrise what it seemed. The world is going into random degeneration, like a worn-out Nuclear Power station.

'Do you believe in Euthanasia?'

'Being homosexual's not *that* bad,' he replies.

Not so much a sunrise as a burn-out; as if the sky were having one last fling before disappearing altogether.

I hurry back to tell Mummy about the Northern Lights. See, the world still has Sights to Unfold.

She preempts me by asking if I am having a problem with my bowels.

'No.'

Then what took me twenty minutes back there?

'I was talking to the Steward, about the Northern Lights, which you can see if you lean over towards me like this.'

Now that you are married, she says, you must not talk to strange men in dark toilets.

'He's homosexual.'

He needs help, then, in her opinion, like Gloria had, in a psychiatric hospital. They had an affinity with public toilets, she informs me.

I shall not enter into a discussion of how 'public' the toilets are this high over the Atlantic.

What tribe describes these lights as celestial beads thrown around the North Pole for a wedding necklace? I should join that tribe.

Tell me about the good times, she asks.

'What good times?'

Well, there were good times, and you tell it so well, in your letters, and when you talk, so just tell me about it all one last time before . . .

Physical struggle, theological stress, the request for a gruesome sort of Help, and now this. It had to come out, and it will. I just have time to get the sick bag out of the netting holster of the seat in front and open it. I nearly fill it I think. Mummy screams, on cue, and the Walloped One (it has to be, doesn't it?) comes running.

'I'm alright,' I manage to gurgle, 'she's just worried.' The bag, full of undigested Air Canada food and too much alcohol and a final tot of vodka, I hand gingerly to the waiting stewardess, who smiles a ghastly smile as she takes it.

Why *does* it have to be her? I feel as though between us we have assaulted her doubly – my mother with an arm, and I with this vomit. I hate to make enemies so effortlessly.

6   Count Down

So long as I can keep talking, she will not point out the drugs, will not reinterpret Gloria's version of the pharmacy in the light of the conspiracy she thinks she has obtained from me. Surprising what you can do when you have to. I may be able to prevent it; I may find some reason. Or some reason, in the collapsing helix of my thoughts, may present itself, why she should go on living.

The Northern Lights give a last dance, last burst, and fizzle out, and we are left in the glow of concealed cabin lights. Through this gloom passes the pilot presently with a screwdriver towards the darkened toilets at the back. He is definitely drunk. Either that, or the first, insidious symptoms of my mother's illness are creeping up on him.

Only the trouble is, images of sadness and disintegration swamp me at the moment. Like a person told to cheer up, to 'smile, it won't happen', I am overwhelmed with glumness. I must go back down into the past and find some moments of illumination or of peace. Perhaps it would be as well to think of this as a humorous endeavour; after all, tragedy is only comedy turned inside out. As if I were about to run backwards a film of chimneys being blown up, seeing them rise gracefully from their own dust into perfect alignment, brick by brick.

How can I say about her childhood, when I have only the bitter-sweet myths of my grandmother to go on? When pressed beyond resistance, she would tell stories

52

more or less consistent, more or less reliable, and, I'm sure, true in their own way. My mother denies most of it, as if she would deny her origins because the world was trying to denigrate her individuality by giving her an ordinary birth, a simple start.

So, were I to refer to her birth as the only survivor of twins, in a dingy Blackheath tenement to a Catholic couple on the verge of separation, named Charlotte but called Charlie after the dead twin, Charles, spoilt rotten, the youngest of four, brought up by a mother who, despite her own lack of education, could still recite most of *King Lear* when I was ten, she would only say, 'Oh, I don't think so. Not really.'

And if I were to repeat the story told me of the siblings all doing handstands against the sitting-room wall one winter evening in the Blackout when the lights failed and Gloria screamed, and they all laughed, only she went on screaming when the lights were restored because it was appendicitis, she would probably say, 'not exactly, not quite.'

Even though the tinted brown-on-brown photographs are there to prove it, and Gloria is still screaming for help.

So I'll have to run the film fast-forward to my own birth, or to my memories, so that there can be no doubt. In fast-forward, then, my lens skims over the image of the three sisters (Babs, Gloria and Charlie) lounging suggestively against each other, smoking Woodbines, smiling outside a sweet-shop on the Seven Sisters' Road; my mother's jacket open, tie skew-whiff, attitude rebellious before teenagers were a named group to be reckoned with.

Here is a black card on the screen with white letters: 'and now . . . the Bad Influence'; see Beryl, the nursing pal, with a shock of long black hair and a mobile face. She can move her ears and wiggle her nose. They move together in the jerky half-light of silent black-and-white through maternity wards, laughing at the naughty bits, with rakish white paper caps.

53

Then the film darkens, Beethoven beats ominously in the background, dots appear again, presaging this time, 'The Meeting' with my father, dying. This is a scene from those sentimental silents with heroines whose names are flowers, whose eyelids are kohled and flickering. He is dying of tuberculosis: she, the sweet nurse whose very sweetness delivers him.

The mad doctor in the white coat, thinning beard, newly-available National Health wire-framed spectacles, is giving live vaccine on this side of the ward, dead vaccine on that. The organ music rises to a crescendo. Which will our sunken-eyed hero be? The Lucky or the Unlucky?

Dawn rises and one side of the ward are curled into grotesque spasms of death, the other side, my now Notdying Dad-to-be one of them, are well and smiling (perhaps they cannot see the corpses on the other side of the ward?).

The music is Air on a G-string. Swiftly my mother walks down the aisle, swiftly as the music changes to the syncopation of Here Comes the Bride played too fast, cantering down the aisle with him of whom we no longer speak, his promise on the rails again: the altar rails. And then the resounding of a Cambridge College choir spirals and revolves up the ancient walls of the round church. The groom is thin as a streamer in morning suit; the bride plump and powdered according to the fashion of the day. The aunts of the groom have slid their camphorous, furled hats from dusty tissue paper in the bottom drawers of oak chests in the front rooms of their stone cottages in Barnoldswick, near Colne. They have come down by train. They wear arched shoes they could never wear on the cobbles at home. Uncle Owen ruins the photograph afterwards by being over seven foot tall and too distant a cousin to be stood at the bottom front of the church steps. The two sides of the event, North and South, had difficulty understanding each others' vowels and gave up. They were never, in any case, to meet again, this side of death. Centuries of division were

54

not healed by this marriage; if anything, the rift widened.

The Northern contingent were overwhelmed by the impossible hope that their semi-orphaned collective son – loved by a dozen childless couples, object of a thousand offers of wise advice – was striving from the cobbled gutters, from the very jaws of death, to the heights of academia, and beyond. And what lay beyond? Impossible to imagine. How can people with no indoor plumbing whatsoever imagine such wealth and success?

'And now . . . The Result', in the very next frame, confetti still visible on the studio floor (or is it the age of the film?), she is pregnant with me, her baby-face full of post-war optimism and British Pluck. Here we can finally freeze-frame for a moment and slow down the rapid flicker, as I arrive on the scene, dragged forth by an ancient forceps, the dent from which I carry over my left eyebrow to this day.

All this passes through my mind as the Northern Lights shatter and fade, and colour leaves the horizon like the dying down of a firework. For the control-test of whether my mother's illness alone is responsible for her present plight lies solely in the events of the past, before the onset of the illness, which I can verify.

Only, the trouble is, images of sadness and disintegration swamp me at the moment.

She wants to hear what she already knows, writ as Good Times. It is 'tell me the one about . . .' not 'tell me a story'. Children thrive on these oft-told tales; so long as the telling is word-perfect, for the telling is a comfort in itself; it is the purpose of Legend and Myth. The enigma is that any new story ever emerges.

She wants to draw strength from the story – her present is all one gruesome warp, the past another weft. The telling will fuse the two-ply together, and strengthen

55

her. Perhaps. It is really the least I can do, whether or not it is a dying wish.

'For me the story begins with an oxygen tent full of London Fog in 1952: the Year of the Smog, the year when I was at the mercy of your heroism: in the middle of the main road, in your arms, in the grip of pneumonia.'

She was racing against time and she knew she was because she was a Trained Nurse, and knew just how short a time it takes for a baby to die, racing to get me to Great Ormond Street and the oxygen tent, before I died. The Smog made purposefulness impossible, it must have done. She must have gripped me tight, swaddled no doubt against the bitter cold, barely breathing, surrounded by invisible traffic, the horns muffled by the thick air. And she didn't know which way to walk, having lost all sense of direction in the middle of the road. Up and down; left and right; perhaps gravity had stopped. Finally she was shouting 'Help! Help!' into the murky air until someone heard, probably a blind person who had not noticed any change in the street, and led us out through the gap in gravity to the hospital. We'll never know who saved us. I kept them guessing for a week and then recovered. Why? Why, against the odds? It must have been the strength of her determination, and mine.

But if she had been knocked down in that Smog, or given up, or fainted? Oh Mummy, just me and you in a fierce and hostile universe, sun, moon, and stars obliterated. At Death's door and *refusing* to enter. Not yet. But for her, it might have been better, to have died then, seeing what was to come. The present so embitters the past.

This I must pass over: we do not need to know *how* Hansel and Gretel came to *be* stepchildren, or their parents *that* poor. Some things are 'given' in every story. 'Given that' we say, as if we really thought the pattern of our lives, however baleful, a divine gift.

56

'Remember going to choose a new council flat in Stoke Newington?'

Brand new building: just a shell. Two maisonettes high, four stories in all, with the sky still visible from railings through to the ground-floor gardens. Surrounded by allotments-to-be and a reservoir with swans. We stumbled over the builders' rubble to look through a letter-box at the doorless first floors. They hadn't yet planted the baby trees in their wire cages in the courtyard, there were not yet chalk marks for ball games on the sheer side of honey-coloured brick at the end. But most of all, there were not yet any people, just the pre-ghosts of them, for someone was there telling us that all the ground-floor ones had gone, and any hope of a garden with them.

We were privileged, because of my father's tuberculosis: we were not all to sleep in the same room, so we had priority. But obviously they had considered the number of bedrooms, three, before anything else, because in no other way did we fit in. We were not Jewish for a start. Not even slightly Jewish. Also since my father was a graduate student and then a junior lecturer at King's College, I could not give my four-year-old colleagues any coherent sense of the 'job' my father did, for it was beyond my own understanding. People there worked in the rag-trade, were postmen, policemen, car salesmen, nurses. None of them were Cambridge graduates, none of them were the children of intellectuals. Hence, perhaps, they taunted me with the Yiddish they could 'speak fluently' and the exclusive nature of their faith. You can never be Jewish, no matter how hard you try.

And Nanny, who lived with us, was even more out of place. She who had ridden to school in a pony trap with the governess, who had been the poor relative of people with titles.

She was there to look after me while my mother worked at Great Ormond Street as a ward sister. So it was Nanny who cooked and cleaned and took me to

57

ballet and the park and was 'far too lenient' all round, especially when I had that dream about the dogs snarling in the small square room, my first on my own, and went in to her and was allowed, secretly, to snuggle there all night.

But even at six and seven I became aware that my mother, though not my far *more* educated father, regarded my grandmother, my substitute mother, with contempt.

If Nanny wanted to keep me off school with a cold my mother would forbid it, accusing Nanny not only of sheer ignorance of Matters Medical but also of conspiring to make an invalid of me. If a child could not get to school through illness, that child ought to be in hospital. If my mother heard me shouting about those dogs in the night she would storm in and tell me to go to sleep instantly. Nanny, the ignorant woman with No Education, would say the right thing, if it was her. Yes, I can see the dogs, but dogs are nice, they won't hurt you and I'll tell them to go away. Nanny lived in a world of ignorance, superstition, fanciful notions of illness and a Fear of Damp pervaded her reasoning, but everything she did and said was informed by one overriding concern: me. And in that lay more security than in all the Positive Materialism and common sense based on Medical Research which my mother could come up with.

It was no wonder my mother must have thought she was fighting a losing battle for supremacy over me.

Once my father joined in with this battle. I was sitting on his lap in the sitting room of our maisonette. We were looking through a large nature book from the library. I know now about such books. I always look up something in the index now and turn two pages at once. But then, I didn't know and so it was a complete shock when one moment I was looking into the eyes of a Beatrix Potter of a mole, a sweet rodent face, and the next, the page slicing over, through the vision; it was a spider, blown up to the size of a puppy. I screamed with fear and ran away. I stood out in the hall, crying, just enough presence of mind to listen to the adults, shouting inside the room.

– What have you done to her, you stupid woman! Stupid, superstitious women. She has learnt this fear, learnt it from you. No-one is born afraid of spiders. You and your stupid mother! What seemed the strangest to me was the unhappy 'lumping' together of the two generations, for I could never imagine what they had in common.

– Perfectly healthy disgust, my mother was answering back. Predatory, unnatural beasts. Why put them in such books for children? No one likes insects, it's instinctive. I haven't taught her anything of the kind.

And so on. I should have been reassured when my father told me later that I had learnt a phobia, that it was not my own phobia. I shouldn't have been afraid of tomatoes with their spider-hats, and then tomatoes without, but I was. I should have been able to walk under the big one which spun a canopy over the cement stairwell to the ground floor each time I had to walk down the stairs, and then any stairs, and then any high places. But I wasn't. And the more irrational, brainless, half-witted, illogical, cretinous and moronic this fear was demonstrated to be, the more of a hold it had over me.

'Those were golden days, Mum. Swans and roller skates in the yard, and my first two-wheeler. And Philip shouting "Snails, men!" though we were all girls. We would follow him at a gallop anywhere, though usually across the road to the posh houses to root in the undergrowth for slimy pets.'

She smiles. Actually she forbade us to go there at the time. And the Superintendent (a man who dressed up like a policeman and was once seen to spit at his own shadow) forbade us to chalk lines on the neverendingly high wall in the courtyard, but how else could you play Donkey?

'There was a Fancy Dress competition for all the children in the flats.'

You were Little Bo Peep, my mother says, I made the costume.

'That's right. I remember it: a bonnet from cardboard and crepe paper, a crook out of a coat hanger with bias binding wrapped around it and a ribbon under the question mark, and a long wide skirt with splash patterns of yellow and blue which was yours, with Nanny's shawl and apron. Did I have a sheep? I can't remember. A tin of toffees was the prize, given by a policeman, or a vicar, or . . . a man in uniform. Oh, we were walking on air with the tin of toffees past the reservoir with the swans, up the stairs, to tell Nanny, "I've won, I've won!" '

She frowns at this. Why?

'Was I six or seven? Thomas hadn't yet been born, I think.'

Thomas's birth was an important landmark of those times. Suddenly all theological questions were swept aside because I had the Asset which surpassed even a spare pair of roller skates – the Baby Brother. And then, even better, the Baby Toddler.

Her frown is fixed, furrowing, intense.

What is it here? Something frightening lurks. Go back down round the helix and see, back out the door, having told Nanny, walk backwards past the railings where people were rumoured to have fallen, not looking at the cement walls where spiders dwell, down the cement stairs, past the muddy water with swans, behind the diamond-shaped thousand-foot-high wire fence, and to the Fancy Dress Parade, where I am the centre of attention, and being photographed, or rather, Little Bo Peep is being photographed.

Deborah is a witch, Sherman a cowboy, Catherine and her quiet sister are hula-hula dancers, a strange tall girl is a Flower Fairy.

Keep going. Back further.

Earlier still, as this costume was being pinned on to me . . . hold still . . . keep . . . ah yes. The evening before all this I went as usual to Catherine's flat below ours (they

60

had a garden and a swing) – a would-be ballet dancer with bright legs and a large mouth, who had run past the camera on one of the first BBC Schools programmes (on the Industrial Revolution) with her hair knotted and greased. It had taken her mother a week to wash it out. Her mother, who was flapping and motherly and fat and 'rather common', shared with my mother only the distinction of *not* being Jewish.

The flat was astrew with raffia. Mr Shore was always buried under some activity of his wife and daughters' – nowhere to be seen, hardly accountable. We are making skirts for the Fancy Dress, Jane. Come in. Give me a kiss. What Fancy Dress, Mrs Shore? She gave her elder, quiet daughter a Knowing Look. So they haven't told you? What? I have a catsuit for you, sweetie, come tomorrow morning and try it on. You *shall* enter. Why should we let *them* win everything?

Oh great, wonderful. I sped up the stairs two at a time, never minding the spiders for once and burst into our kitchen to tell everyone that Mrs Shore . . .

But I had got it All Wrong. No daughter of hers was wearing a cheap catsuit to a Fancy Dress, and who did Mrs Shore think she was anyway? I was made to go back down the stairs, now thick with monstrous spiders, to tell Mrs Shore very politely, that I would not be needing the catsuit after all, thank you, and then straight to bed – from where I could hear the raised voices of my mother and grandmother seemingly far into the night.

The next morning, there was the outfit. She must have spent the whole night making it. More threatening than Fancy, more aggressive than Fun: I wore it, entered in it, was photographed in it, and won.

Catherine Shore was furious and kept snapping the elastic holding her coconut halves onto her flat chest in anger.

Common as muck; I ask you: hula girls!

The prize was bad for your teeth; I only had one.

* * *

61

'Why *are* you frowning, Mummy?'

How could I have been so cruel, she is saying, moved to tears all this time afterwards, how *could* I?

'What then? What did I do?'

Asked that dreadful woman to provide a catsuit for me, as if my own mother wouldn't make me something, like everyone else.

Ah, I see.

7   Stars and Stripes

The Walloped One is in Fancy Dress: it is an outfit which tries at one and the same time to outline with unnecessary detail the ample curves of her body, thus enticing the close interest of the male Passenger, and yet does so by means of a *suit*, thus reassuring the female Passenger that she is Serious, Responsible and Professional.

This contradictory outfit is coming slowly towards us. She is approaching people, pointing to the hand luggage they have stowed above their heads on the sloped shelves and getting them to remove it. You'd think it would be worth their while to install lockers! When she gets to us, I am ready to retrieve Mummy's overnight bag, no doubt full of imitation jewellery and twenty types of talcum powder, but she stops before she reaches us, swivels and returns back down the aisle as if we didn't exist.

'This is discrimination, Mummy. Aren't we entitled to be told off, too?'

My mother says, with mock sadness, that she is probably intimidated by my rudeness, or my vomit.

'I wasn't rude. You *hit* her!' We giggle. I hope she can hear us, waggling back down the plane.

'Even you couldn't have foreseen that we were about to undergo something of a culture shock then, from London council flat to mansion on millionaire's row of the Santa Barbara Riviera? From drizzle perpetual, cement and asphalt, to sunshine, sea and cactus!'

People living outdoors all year round, where we had

dashed from one indoors to the next, our faces tickled by woollen balaclavas, our noses dripping continually, coughing on the windswept stairways a familiar sound of home.

Now home was a Spanish-style mansion on the Riviera of Santa Barbara, overlooking the mission below, and the bright, bright sea. Behind the ornate shutters which kept out the intense light of the Californian sky from the fadeable chintz covers of the imitation English antique furniture, my mother sniggered jealously about the millionaireness of millionaires, about their frequent changes of husband, their obviousness, their ostentation.

The little boy next door asked my father one day on the flagstoned patio, something about King Arthur. My father looked up from his paper, not having heard him distinctly, and said, 'Sir?' for him to repeat the question.

– Sorry, I mean Sir Wells. From then on the two children from the house with the swimming-pool next door called my father Sir Wells.

My mother said they were 'underprivileged' children, for although they had a swimming-pool they never saw their mother, who was always on the point of a Mexican divorce, followed by a Californian marriage. A full-time live-in Spanish maid looked after them. What is underprivileged about that, I wondered, sitting in their rosewood and Spanish-tiled kitchen, drinking buttermilk and eating home-made cookies. She thought I was too thin and that Sir and Lady Wells did not know how to 'feed up' children. Not to tell your mother please, though.

He, of whom we no longer speak, went swimming on Christmas Day just to be photographed doing so for the family album. Holding the newspaper precariously above the surf and pointing to the indecipherable date, like some victim of a kidnap, proving he is still alive, rather than a young historian on a year's secondment from an English university. A strange fish indeed in that just pre-Beachboy era, thin and pale and English: a flat cap of blond hair over bony and sunken features of a long face recently hospitalized. Californian faces are wide open and brown with the sun; if they are blond, it is either peroxide (Marilyn Monroe's corpse was bald, my mother informs us, on account of the peroxide) or the action of the sun on chestnut hair wet from the surf, not Norse-blond, stone-blond, grey, English essential blond.

My mother's appearance too was at odds with the surroundings, though in her case it was deliberate. Her make-up was a strict business – simply a vicious and accurate drawing on of two lemon-slice shapes with bright red lipstick over her thin lips. Nothing else was permitted. Eye make-up, so beloved of Americans, was simply outrageous, tarty. As were fringes. My mother's short black wavy hair was *swept* away from the face – to where it belonged, on the head – and kept there with a little judicious oil. Her eyebrows were unplucked, fierce, black and sparse. It is, I know now, a well-known English type: the district nurse with her sensible flat shoes and her unpainted face. Nothing to excess, nothing frivolous.

'Remember the garden? Fantastic plants toppling over a precipitous slope down to the bottom of the Riviera? Rocks the size of small cars, with strange lizards twitching on them. You could live outdoors, in a state of rapture.'

– Can Jane come to the beach with us? asked Susan from next door.

– No, she has homework to do.

– Then we'll wait while she does it, said Susan, stubborn and unused to being denied anything.

We went to Santa Monica in the old station-wagon, the third car, which was always full of sand. At the very yellow-livered edge, where a non-swimmer like myself was obliged to stand, watching them dip and reappear in the foam, I felt safe. Then the next instant they had all gone somewhere, the beach was empty, the sky empty and quiet and cloudless. The moment stretched open and I looked in front of me, realizing *it was not sky.*

There was a wall as high as a skyscraper in front of me, like the glass side of a vast fishtank. Fish and starfish and seaweed and stones moved slowly upward to the top of this wall through the water, bright green. Ah! Beautiful, I thought, so be. . . . I regained consciousness on the beach a few seconds later. Maria had turned me upside down and thumped me on the back and was jabbering in Spanish.

– Why dintcha move? Why dintcha move outta the way? asked Susan.

Out of what way? I had not lost my footing, joined the wall, flipped, and gone under; I had simply stayed there and been knocked out by the force of the wall hitting me.

– What was it?

– A wave, y'dummy! Just a wave? Outrageous to have such waves: excessive, ridiculous. Knocked out by a wave at the water's edge. How is it possible?

You shall not go to the beach with them again. They are not responsible.

I was already bent on escape, though. I went to the bottom of our long, downwards garden on the edge of the Riviera, miles and miles from the top, from the civilised bit. I had gone down through the strata: through the rough grass and wild flowers, through the tundra of gorse bushes and stones, through the bare speckled rock and down to the very bottom where there was nothing but white sand, the hot, stretched highway, and the sea beyond. I had reached the desert, the no man's land.

I did hear, from far, far above me, my mother's voice not frantic, not worried, but angry, shouting for me.

'Jane-ey-ey!'

It would be a long climb back up and I had just arrived at the bottom. I tried shouting back, but whereas her voice floated down, perfect in every brutal cadence and nuance, mine would not take wing up the precipice. My words flapped back down into my face.

I couldn't think, then, why she was so anxious for me

to come back up. But I know now that she was afraid I would repeat the Great Escape of a few weeks before.

'It's not true to say council flat to mansion, though, is it? First we lived in that dreadful pre-fab, with "areas" instead of rooms, where I had to go to the Grey School.'

My mother is trying to correct me, wrapping her wayward tongue around the word 'bungalow' and trying to say 'the Grade School'.

'Bungalow, then. The name makes it no less awful. Rows of cardboard bungalows in a small grey desert with a grey box in the middle denoting a school I had to attend, where I stood every morning hand on heart (literally) saying "I pledge a Legion to the United States and the Public upon which it stands . . ." in all my Britishness.'

My mother is giggling now, she says she is remembering how I told them that I would be shot if I didn't say the Pledge, when she and my father suggested I just kept silent.

Well, really, it seemed to me that they had got it *all* slightly wrong – cars the size of 'trailers', the 'faucets' too far apart, the sky bigger, the people too large and racially ambiguous. As if the whole project were based on a plan since lost and only partially recalled.

When I said, on that first morning, that I wanted to go home, and not to the Grey School, standing by the entrance to the miles and miles of unlandscaped dust surrounding the weatherboarded, one-storied box of a school, it was not so much a request, as a statement of terror. At eight I had only just begun to master Stoke Newington, this new planet was too much too soon.

'There were no desks, but there was Social Studies, Spanish, and a lesson called Recess. "I guess so" could mean "I may be wrong" or "Isn't it obvious?" depending on the context, only I had no way whatsoever of understanding any of the contexts. A half-Spanish girl deputed to look after me guessed that there would be no school dinner.'

How could we have known? asks my mother.

'I'm not blaming you. But you did tell me there were no such things as Monsters.'

Nothing could have prepared me for them, in any case: slow, fat people in the middle of the dust of no or any age, milling around with their arms dangling oddly by their sides, their faces distorted and their lips dribbling. These are just our Re-Tards, Jane. Oh, that's what they are, is it? Sometimes a label is less useful than an abscessed wisdom tooth on a Bank Holiday Weekend.

And Nanny wasn't there to say she could see them, that they wouldn't hurt me, and that she would tell them to go away.

It was the same problem in the maths lesson. The teacher asked me and asked me what was the difference between eight and thirteen. I didn't know. I could have subtracted one from the other, had she taken the trouble to explain the word, the concept. But she kept on with her label-question, 'What is the difference?' Finally I said, 'One can be written continuously without taking the pencil from the page, and the other can't.' I thought this was a good difference. She thought I was taking the piss, had obviously never heard of lateral thinking (neither had I – it hadn't been invented yet) and punished me. The punishment was to stand in the playground dust and watch the Re-Tards watching me, gradually closing in to have a look at my long blonde plaits.

You were so bright, was the trouble, my mother is saying, we had you moved to another class with ten-year-olds.

No, that was not the trouble.

'Well, I remember thinking, I won't be staying here long enough for it to matter. It was only temporary, a few days at most. Like the bungalow; even the Monsters perhaps were temporarily there from another planet. Hadn't the Americans begun to explore the possibility of exploring the moon, after all? Or were they from a mental asylum? Did you become one after temporarily being normal? Perhaps the Re-Tards were the *graduates*, what this type of schooling turned you into?'

My mother laughs now, she has seen the funny side.

Down the helix, though: the Great Escape.

Okay, so I don't know the proper passwords, and sleep at the wrong times of day and night because of the jet-lag. But I'm not staying. Forever on my newly-allowed bare feet, I shall walk away. The Baby has learnt to say 'uh-huh' in ten different ways in order to express all his needs and reactions. Perhaps Tommy will not need to learn to speak now? Can he graduate to Re-Tardness without intervening schooling?

The bungalow had no rooms, just areas: sleeping areas, TV areas, kitchen areas and so on. We argued from our different areas, having slept at the wrong times, about whether it was called the Grade School or the Grey School.

I just wandered out, past an enormous bowl of oranges. The walking was dreamy and unreal, and the dream of Home was real enough to smell.

For, surely, I can just walk down this dust track and find myself on Blackheath or Lewisham High Street. It's only a mock-up of some sort.

Past the bowl of oranges. In England we bought oranges one at a time; here they come like apples, by the sackful.

At the far end of the track, which ran between the rows of huts, abruptly the desert of sand-dust finished and on top of it, as if just placed there like plasticine on a sandpit, is a pavement. Someone has just *put* the road there. At home the roads are part of the landscape, resting on earlier roads, but *this* street, put there the week before last? Yesterday? And why there, rather than anywhere else? Might they change their minds tomorrow? Over there would be better; let's move it, shall we?

Let's move everything; let's start all over again.

* * *

There I stood, eight years old in white tennis shorts and a pale blue aertex shirt, barefoot, staring at the lights flashing on a cinema opposite and no-one seemed to notice. Was I invisible? Had I stood thus in Catford High Street, even on such a hot, dark night as this, someone would have come up to me and asked me what I thought I was up to.

'We used to laugh about the traffic being all wrong; the buses being too short and their doors opening, people pouring out and more surging in, without there ever having been a queue. How did they know who had been there first, you used to say. It offended your sense of order and civilised behaviour.'

It still does, she says, in Canada.

I could not cross the road. I didn't know the passwords for that. It was just as well, since I stayed on the same side, walking, and watching the people.

'And the people seemed so strange; they walked as if they were always just out for a stroll, not as if they were ever going anywhere.'

Even the stars were more intersected with wires and cables, because nothing went underground, or deep. Stars and stripes: everything temporary.

'Everything there, obvious, showing.'

All the inwards, outwards: spread across the sky.

I was far, far from home.

They must have panicked. Strange house, street, town, country, continent – late, late at night because I had slept at the wrong time. A dreamy, unreliable child of eight, walking barefoot around a suburb of Los Angeles.

And there came a point when I ceased escaping and knew that I was lost.

No, I said later, it was not homesickness made me do it. At eight you cannot say exactly what it is that impels you to walk past the oranges out into the night. Relief must have muted their anger. I remember only the muffled whisper of voices between the areas and a sound like a balloon popping by the front door.

But I realize now that she feared I had gone again when, standing at the bottom of the garden in the sandy dirt, with rocks and paths towering over me, her voice intensified to a scream and was shortly afterwards joined by my father's voice. I started to climb then.

Of course, she screamed because she could not climb down the cliff after me. Her balance must have been already impaired. She would have to scream.

'Do you remember when Tommy drove the car away, on the slope outside the Riviera house?'

Only one and a half and he went out, got into the car, let off the handbrake and sailed away down the road 'steering'. A tree must have stopped him, or a lamp-post and when he was carried in, blood was pouring from his eye. Everyone panicked but her. He'll be blind, he'll die, I thought. But she simply wiped and wiped at the blood, silently and then announced that it was only the eyelid, which was very 'vascular'. Such calm. The real catastrophes never fazed her.

It was only a lot of blood, my mother replies, bridling her crooked little self into an even worse posture, you were all such ninnies about it.

But she's pleased, I can tell.

That house, shuttered continually in my memory, as if against bad weather which never happened. A house designed inside on the Hollywood model, as a set to frighten people. One of the bedrooms was the one the owner's husband had 'recently' died in, so Susan told me. Do you dare to go in and lie on the bed? Why not? Because you will be *snatched*, if you do. By whom? The Holy Ghost, of course. How do you know? I go to confirmation classes.

I asked my parents why we didn't use that bedroom. We don't need it, said my mother. But Tommy and I sleep in the same room. Is it because of the Death? No, I'm sure they've disinfected it, said my father. Don't be silly – you can't *catch* cancer: your father is thinking of where he was brought up where people died of flu. They did not. Unsanitary conditions. They were not.

So Tommy and I shared a room. The door must be open a crack. Tommy is ritualled to sleep somehow by my father. I have forgotten the rituals.

– Cover my leaving by turning over, Jane, he whispers. Tommy must not know he has gone. But he will know in the morning; and yet that never bothers him.

It becomes another part of the ritual, my turning over as the crack of light narrows to a thin rod. Rustling to cover his leaving. Why is it never my mother who pulls the door to? At that moment of turning, rustling, letting go, I miss her the most. Not *my* mother; *her* mother.

Sometimes thoughts of home, badly remembered, already fading, would anchor me too firmly in consciousness and I would wait for Tommy's breathing to regularize and slip out of bed. All the floors were carpeted – an unthinkable luxury in those days. I could walk silently to the heavy carved door (in the Spanish style) and through it without making a sound. Along the corridor I could hear low voices. Their door is ajar. My mother is standing in profile to me, before the full-length glass on its own easel by the side of the dressing table. She is wearing a black dress, taffeta, with ruching under the breasts, tightly sucked in at the waist and describing the hips and buttocks lavishly. A small necklace of moonstones in a black setting. She applies the fierce red lipstick, slowly, and chews on her lips. My father is sitting beyond her with a newspaper in front of him. She powders her nose from a compact and clicks it shut. She turns and smoothes her hands down over her rump. Her calves bulge under the scalloped hem of the dress, a seam marks the perfect bisection of the muscle. Her feet are squeezed into black shoes with a two inch heel on them, patent.

– Is anything showing? she asks my father. He says something inaudible about Nixon. Is Charlie dead? she says. It's her joke – is Charlie dead, is the petticoat showing? He puts down the paper.

– Very nice, dear, fine. What time are we expected?

She sits and staples some large round earrings into place under her small ears. They wink evilly under her severe black crop.

– Ten minutes ago, she says.

– Are we late, then?

– No, Maria isn't here yet and I don't want to be the first; it's so vulgar to be the first and we'd have to drink so much gin before the meal.

I creep back along the spooky panelled corridor and that transformation glitters through all the black-edged mirrors of my dreams.

The year's teaching, lecturing, being dined and fêted, came to an end and it wasn't yet time to go 'home'. I heard for the first time about Income Tax, and camping. The two are inextricably linked in my mind. Because of Income Tax, hence Camping. We had to stay out of the country (ours) for some months more. So, naturally, we undertook a gruelling journey from California up the West Coast of the United States, to Canada. In high summer, in a wreck of an English car, and with Tommy still in nappies.

I say naturally – but what could be more unnatural? Mary Kingsley warned travellers in Nigeria always to filter their water, to eliminate dead crocodiles and humans. She travelled in long skirts. All I can say is that she and my parents must have shared some kind of peculiarly English recklessness, or optimism.

'Do you remember the camping, Mum?'

One of the highpoints of my life, she says.

High points? It's true – in extremis, she flourished. The whole journey was a series of comic-strip disasters and spectacular visions – of Yellowstone Park, the

73

Grand Canyon, the Rockies, the deserts and towns which seemed to be only one room deep along dirt roads with two petrol pumps and a bank between the two signs, 'Welcome to . . .' and 'Goodbye. Drive Carefully Now!' at either end of the main street.

Through this land of extremes, of frying heat and bone-snapping cold, we drove and drove. We never knew whether a mishap would be sufficiently absurd for my mother to burst out laughing, or frustrating enough to arouse her anger. So we became wary, us in the back, one with nappies and one without, expiring from the heat or huddling together for warmth.

'We did our best to do America, didn't we?'

We succeeded, she remonstrates, stroking her chin with her wrist, the hand having flopped down. The gesture is a childish one – wiping dribble off with a sleeve end. It reminds me of something. Bears.

'Mum – remember that bear?'

Oh yes. She makes to give herself a bear hug, nails digging into the turquoise. Oh, yes.

Soft pine-needle floor and darkness from the giant trees: at the bottom you are under the dark side of the moon, though bright day is above. Bears we know about – but never see; surely they are Paddington, Pooh, Edward bears?

Our tent is at half-mast, my father has Tommy in among the guy ropes, a fleshy bundle flapping joyfully in the chaos. My mother sways over to the trash-can with our garbage and supports herself on the side of the bottom one-millionth of a sequoia tree. She has no free hand; she removes the bearproof lid of the trash-can with an upward jerk of her knee.

Crash.

One of the massive trunks, a house wide, a mountain high, starts to move into the clearing. Brown on brown – a shape moves into the half-light of the clearing and forms itself into fur and eyes and claws.

Should any camper be molested by a bear, the rule is

this: freeze, do not move. When vacating Yellowstone
Park, report the incident to the Ranger, who will ask you
to identify the bear, so that its rear end may be painted
red. Only what happens in between freezing and
vacating?

We froze. Except Tommy who continued rolling and
squealing until my father pinned him down by virtually
squatting on him. The action of 'freezing' made my
mother's swaying more pronounced than usual.

The tower of fur moved towards the trash-can. He
stirred the contents with one daggered paw, sniffing.
He kept his eyes on my mother. I could see his face and
hers.

Fear. Animals can smell it, they say.

Try to think of something else.

Stirring, stirring.

– Steady yourself, my father whispered to her. But
she could not. I suddenly panicked for her. She will fall.
The bear will be frightened and attack her.

A century passed, a century of panic and fear. The
joints of my knees stiffened and trembled. Tommy cried
out. The bear turned towards the odd grouping of man
and baby. My father moved so that the bear could not
see Tommy, he was completely covered.

Oh no, eat her, eat her. Not Tommy, please.

A car passed on the road. The bear collapsed onto all
fours and galloped back into the brownness.

– Describe the bear, sir.
  – How? All bears look the same.
  – Yerr kidding.
  – To me they do.
  – Did it have a red bum?
  – No.
  – Then you were in no danger.

No danger? Now she remembers the *sense* of danger
with a delicious wiggle of the upper arms. Fearing to
lose a life which was precious, promising. So the Good

75

Times are really the Worst Moments, when the promise of Good Times was real.

I was the one who had the nightmares; magic circles in evil woods with my mother at the centre, swaying, falling, the bear stirring her around in the pine-needles, and a force-field prevents any of us from entering, to help her. But I could help her if I was prepared to risk my life and step into the magic zone. I cannot raise the courage, in my nightmares, and the bear consumes her as I watch, rooted.

'Thank God for Nivea tins, eh Mum? They probably don't make them like that any more. Probably plastic now.'
    She laughs, remembering.

We were climbing into the very sky, up into the thin air, up the Rockies. The Ford Anglia burst into steam and came to a halt. She stood, arms akimbo, furious, by the raised bonnet accusing my father of navigational and mechanical incompetence and more besides. Hadn't she suggested a better route and predicted this very thing?
    Abruptly her top half was in at the open window. She upended her handbag on the seat and unscrewed the cap of the Nivea cream tin. It fitted the radiator perfectly, so that once again she had Saved the Day, and was Always Right. We continued up the mountains, into a cloud.
    'Great way to see America, from the inside of a cloud.'
    Enough is enough. She must be Right, she always is – so we will camp here even though it is too cold to breathe and the ground is so hard the tent pegs snap as he hammers them in.
    All you two wanted was your chocolate, but it was frozen, she says.
    Tommy cried out with the cold in the night, the damp edges of the tent crystallized into solid sheets. We lit the primus stove at dawn for warmth. Never was the world so still or silent as when we tugged at those tent pegs

until they snapped. Finally we pulled the tent and its integral ground sheet off, and discovered . . .

'We were pitched on a sheet of solid ice; we had spent the night in a natural refrigerator.'

We were in a cloud, and couldn't see what we were doing, she says.

Into Family History, exaggerated into Myth, and told a hundred times, as if it had been High Comedy.

Destination: University of British Columbia Summer School, for the summer.

'In Vancouver you tried to teach me to swim.'

I don't remember that, she says.

Spending a sunshine day by the lake's edge. The house is partly in the water. Expanse of water, of pines under a wide Vancouver sky.

They live in this idyll; we are only visiting. He is a colleague of my father's but they are friends and do not talk shop.

– I can swim faster than my neighbour's motor boat.

– Meccano, is it?

They josh. Josh, josh. Go on, take the boat then. Do you know how to sail? Yes, who doesn't? Coming, Thomas? Be my crew. He is just ten toes and a nose at opposite ends of the orange life-jacket. They set out on the sea of a lake, sails fully open.

She lends my mother a swimsuit, and one of her three daughters lends me one. Come, let's swim. You can hold onto the jetty, Charlotte, if you feel unsteady.

Janey, it's time you learnt to swim – look at these girls! Waist deep she undulates with the wake from the departing sail-boat. I face the other way, out to sea, so to speak. Watching the boat out on the water. I could only just make out their shapes – a tall narrow sitter and a small orange bundle. Now just lean into the water and push your feet off.

Gulp, swallow, burst up.

– No, I hate it!

– I'm determined. Now is the time.

77

A bird passed overhead. I tried again, sank again, gulped and drank the lake and spun back up into the warm air.

A bird screamed over the lake.

– Helll! Helll!

She is angry with me now.

– Will you do as I say?

It was not a bird. The boat has gone. Where has it gone?

– HELP! HELP! The boat was upside down and two figures, one with a lifejacket and one without, were bobbing in the water beside it.

My mother turned finally, in response to my pointing and the look on my face, and shouted a siren of a scream.

He ran past us, along the jetty, picked up a wooden surfboard and dived. His propeller-arms sped the surfboard towards the capsized boat. A motor boat followed a few seconds later, but arrived at the accident *after* the swimmer.

– Your father is exhausted. They laid him on the floor in the sitting room. What does exhausted mean?

It means that a man with one lung and no lifejacket, who feared he would drown his son if he put his weight on the one lifejacket they had, had trod water until he could tread no more, nearly twenty minutes. A bird had flown into the sails of the wooden-ruddered boat and capsized it.

Your son is fine, they keep telling him. But he won't believe it. Almost fine I would say: driving to Montreal he would dive under the seat and close his eyes over bridges, or any expanse of water.

– All gone water, Tommy, you can come up now.

We were standing at a street corner in Montreal, waiting for my father and an uncle to come back with dollars. They were selling a car by driving it around Montreal with a For Sale sign in the window 'no reasonable offer refused', and we were waiting to fly home.

* * *

Meanwhile, someone remarkable was looking down at me, someone with Nanny's features made glamorous and young, someone with clothes of grandeur and fashion, and a deep, melodic voice. Someone who laughed at the story of the Tent Pitched on Ice, and seemed to think Tommy and I belonged to her. An aunt perhaps? The mysterious Aunty Babs, at last?

8 Gatherings

Every so often a hand rises from the ranks of padded head-rests in front of me and switches on a small red light. Shortly the coiffed head of either of the stewardesses or the glossy ear-length locks of the steward bob up to the light, switch it off and confer with the owner of the hand, from above. Why? Are they suffering from bad doggy-dreams and being reassured?

What could grown-ups be needing, in their sleep? Surely all they need now is to arrive, and nothing the uniformed ones can say will advance it. They who spend their working lives fussing around other people's journeys, home or away from home, and back again, in an eternal circle.

Whenever you return from a journey, you are asked, What was it like in America, Africa, Hong Kong? There is no sensible answer to that, unless the person asking has visited for themselves, in which case it would be absurd to ask. The proper question is, 'How do you find England, now that you are back?'

England seemed very strange, when we returned, my mother says, as if she has heard my thoughts – London was so *cold*.

Perhaps she is wondering how she will find it this time, and whether she may still call it Home. For it is a one-way only return this; she may not re-return to Canada if it doesn't suit her. She is not double-entered, she would not be acceptable, I am sure, for immigration, in her condition.

When I hear that Beatles song 'Once there was a way to get back home', I think of our homecoming to Lewisham from the United States. Whatever happened to Stoke Newington?

London. Home is the place where they can't say, because your baby is naked on account of the heat, your father unshaven on account of the camping, and your car on fire with Nivea Fumes, 'We don't care to handle that kind of money in Butte, Montana' and refuse to cash your cheque.

'Yes, very strange, but like home.'

You had missed your grandmother all the time we were away, she says.

'The smell of the garden, with the railway at the end' – of Sunday dinner, suet and custard, the sound of the radio with Nanny singing along to it, or the telephone ringing not buzzing, in the hallway, a distant clatter and the smell of damp, old velvet curtains, a wet cat, and the slight ether-rubber of wellingtons left to sigh and fold over in the hall.

That place was a slum, my mother spits out.

– What are you saying, Nan?
 – There is something wrong with the way she walks; I noticed it at Heathrow.
 – What do you mean?
 – Look at her – she always holds your father's arm.
 – I hadn't noticed.

You don't, do you? That the baby has become a toddler in one year, bilingual, out of nappies, philosophizing about the stars; that you have grown two inches yourself, that the axis of the world has shifted ever so slightly?

'Such a wonderful slum, though, don't you think?'

Coming back from the Riviera of the snazziest (her word at the time) mansions, to a semi in Lewisham with a leaking roof. Only an idyll to a child, I can see that. Its mystery and romance would have been a source of worry and embarrassment to her. Had they made it to the top only to find a snake's head there to slip down?

'For Murder in the Dark, no better place.' Cupboards and small rooms in abundance, and a cellar full of more rooms; rooms which were *for* nothing: coal holes, boxrooms, side-rooms, walk-in cupboards, spare rooms. There were mangles, old radios, rooms with furniture protruding from the walls like sacrificial slabs. There was even a room with no floor next to mine, in the attic.

That place was just a terrible slum, without heating, she repeats.

'Paraffin.' The scent of paraffin everywhere.

– You go up to your room, and stay there. Maybe she'll have walked it off by the time she gets home from work. (Cowering, actually cowering up there in my sweaty blue attic bedroom lined with books) – waiting for the sound of her key in the latch two floors down, and her heavy foot – and – walking-stick – fall on the tiles. And for Nanny's first words to her daughter which she would speak loudly for my benefit up the stairwell, making it clear somehow what was the 'lie of the land'.

– What on earth did you *say* to her, Jane?

– Honestly, Nan, I can't remember.

– You *must* be more careful. You must have said something terrible.

– Not necessarily. You know that.

– I'm not saying anything. Enough has been said in this house already.

Oh, there has been enough said. Her words are arrows and I a sieve.

I was left one afternoon with Tommy, who was only three. I was playing with him in the kitchen. I can see it now. In and out of the alcove, 'Nan's house' and toys on the floor. The afternoon light is streaming in through the kitchen window, next to the door, a stable door with a top half and a bottom half. I wish I could go back now and lock that bottom half, slide the little bolt along into place, make the sunny room safe for the ten minutes my mother is gone. But I can't. I can go in there, hover over the new blue formica units, see the cars and the red fire-engine on the grey linoleum, even smell the disinfectant my mother wiped everywhere. I can look out the window, down into the garden at the fishpond and the grape vine and further, to the railway track. But I cannot draw that bolt. It remains forever, hanging loose.

In a twinkling he must have run at the door and burst it open and pitched headlong down the twelve stone steps onto the concrete below. In a blink of my eyes, or the time it takes to bend and inspect something or switch on the radio. I was only ten but I wouldn't have left him alone even to go to the toilet. And he was gone, the door swinging open onto the stone landing.

I never thought, even in the panic at finding him unconscious and nestling like a baby into a pillow of spreading blood, that I would be *blamed*. Even when my mother was there, lifting, directing me to dial 999 and telling me 'his skull is fractured but he's still breathing' in her clinical, clinical voice, even then, it did not occur to me that I would be blamed. But I was. Once he was home, much stitched, much traumatized, but without, miraculously, any fracture, I was systematically tortured with the accusation, from my mother, and from her alone, that I had neglected him nearly to death and only luck had intervened. I was *never* to be trusted again.

Somewhere in the corner of these memories is the quiet voice of sanity, of my father saying that it could have happened to anybody and he should have fitted a Yale lock.

Nanny came back from Canada and asked how it had happened?

Jane was left in charge of him for five minutes and somehow didn't notice him going out the back door and falling down all twelve steps!

– How did this really happen?
– He fell. It *was* my fault. I should have stopped him.
– How? Are you God?
– I should have known.
– How? Can you read minds? Don't cry, Jane. That boy

83

is reckless, totally reckless, and she knows it. It could have been anyone.

– Tell her! Will you tell her that?

– I have done. Don't you think I have done? She was never left with any of her sisters, never.

– Don't go away again.

– I had to go. Your Aunty Babs was very ill and nearly died.

– I'm sorry. I'm so selfish.

– Now stop it. You're not selfish or wicked or bad. This nonsense has got to stop. You are no different from the rest of us.

Try telling that to the headmistress of my Catholic Prep School; try telling that to the lady who stood by the back door to the cloakrooms while we filed past her off into the garden to the grotto to tell all to Mother Mary. Whether she or her son forgave my negligence I cannot say, because Grace, like electricity, is invisible.

'I suppose, Mum, I went to that school in Blackheath because you had been a Catholic once?'

No, it was for academic reasons, she says, whisking her knuckles curiously over her turquoise skirt as if to brush aside any notions of indoctrination.

Hail Mary full of light, wired from underneath to a small bulb in your plaster moulding, illuminating your blue dress something lovely, forgive me for Tommy's sliced-open head, can you? Imagine if your plaster of Paris fatigued and you dropped that baby? Whose fault would that be? Hail Mary; I am wearing those oversized stamps of cloth with your picture embroidered on them, dangling by a circular ribbon on two sides, which straddle my chest and shoulder blades each night. To ensure easy delivery to the next world. I have the postage on me, don't I? The stamps are there to be seen, under my vest, under the nightie, sticking to my young flesh in the heat of the night, by means I suppose of your X-ray vision. I'm sorry I said 'flesh'. Deliver me from Matters

84

Medical. I want to be entirely invisible, entirely electrical. Forgive me and save me. Not all mothers are like you, Mary, believe me.

– I should have stopped him.

– How? Are you God?

Yes, that. Give me the godpowerful wings to swoop down out of the ceiling space to draw the bolt, to cheat fate of that baby shape at the bottom of the granite steps in the puddle of blood. I had to wait four hours, in a colourless place, staring at the junction of a pipe, not knowing. Is he dead? Is he dead? Is he dead? Surely that is all the punishment a person can endure? That, and knowing that their own mother will never entirely trust them again, forever.

Of course (silly me) that doesn't matter because this world is just a Vale-of-tears, we are reliably informed by the headmistress, along with the basics of algebra. Just an unfortunate waiting room, a bit smelly, defiled, uncomfortable – wherein we must wait patiently for the Death Express which will take us to Valhalla. The place we were trying to get to, destined for, all the time. And to think, we thought this life was the main thing!

The headmistress was an example to us how to wait. She was herself a kind of lay nun. She put lipstick on the inside of her lips (in order not to be provocative, we surmised) while sitting spread-thighed on a high chair before us so that we could examine her curious undergarments, long and frilly. While she read us passages from her brother's long and eventful letters, translated from the Italian, which were an example of How Not to Wait.

The only enduring element of her teaching (and she taught us everything, even gardening, and how to wire up plugs for religious ornaments) was that she told us one day, when we had been tittering unusually obviously about the sight of her underclothes, that soon we would come, through the Grace of God, to regard panties in the

85

same way as any other garment. I have to admit that this moment has not yet arrived for me, even at the time of writing. But I live in hope.

Travelling home on the Blackheath to Lewisham bus was a journey through more than space and time. It was a voyage to another dimension – to atheism, scepticism, druidical superstition and Matters Medical.

Sometimes the dimension was altering visibly as I entered the front door. This surprised me every time. The world may have been a brutal, wobbly, surreal place to me, at eleven; but they must have had a firmer hold on reality. There would be unusual smells from the kitchen. Tommy and I were hurried through a brief tea of bread and honey and fruit, and we would dodge around piles of exotically folded napkins, olives and Tupperware trays, rows and rows of vol-au-vent cases and bowls of tuna-fish paste. Nanny would be rolling and pounding and boiling and putting things on cocktail sticks. There would be tin foil trembling on top of trays, grease-proof buttered and scorched protruding from every bin and box.

– They are giving a party. Your parents know how to throw a good party, Nanny would say, having done all the cooking, bar the lemon mousse (my mother's creation), herself.

My mother, bright red of lip and festoon'd with jewellery, staggered about on heels, sparkling. My father's friends were all academics, hers all medics. But she kept up with everyone. Her wit was crude, and original. I think she did embarrass my father with her dreadful tales of the decapitation of 'locked' twins, of caesarians performed on kitchen tables, in other words, 'shop talk'. Most of her jokes were beyond me – involving obstetricians, letter-boxes, keyholes, rubber gloves. But other adults hooted with laughter and she never missed a break in conversation. There were no silences at their parties, no awkward gaps during dinner. She could always, always think of something to say. My father, on the other hand, would soon be locked into political debate with four black men in the corner of the room, from whence he only emerged to bid the first guests farewell.

I was only on the illicit fringes, of course, supposed to be in bed. Sometimes I could wander in, in my nightie, and charm people. Ah, is this your little girl? Come and have an olive (Never mind the Midas Eyes, the 'I'm warning you') and hear from an old professor how he failed his eleven-plus, and see where it got him! Or a black man with glasses tells me he is a prince from a foreign land, incognito.

So, you would have thought (I would have thought) that given her garrulousness, her Matters Medical, my mother would have coped with the difficult business of explaining about periods to me with less fuss than most mothers. Not so.

'Mummy, I've always wondered, when you said "orange" . . .'

That night the house was quiet. No parties were happening. I was having a nosebleed, as I often did in those days, ironically. It was Brownies night, but I had been expelled the week before for leap-frogging over the plastic model of a mushroom. I had not realized it was as potent a religious icon as Mother Mary. The uniform was being folded up to be given away by Nanny, to someone my mother might deem better behaved and more worthy of it. We were sitting on Nanny's bed. My nose dripped and dripped. I had a pack of ice on the back of my neck, and a bunch of keys held to my forehead and my mother was calming Nanny, telling her that never in the entire world had anyone, absolutely *anyone* died of a nosebleed.

Whether it was the rivers of blood on my school uniform or whether they had planned this little interchange, I don't know, but the subject turned to Other Blood. It went like this: something inside me, *like an orange*, would soon start to drip blood at an appointed time, about every four weeks. It sounded more unlikely than frightening. I thought there was no need, I got rid of enough 'excess blood' through the nose. So perhaps I would be spared. Nanny then said her piece, frowning the while, obviously as puzzled as I was about the orange.

She said that her own mother, Lady Something-orother, had never told her about it and looked into her trunk when she got home one summer and said, 'Oh, you've started to use those, have you?' But I was lucky, because my mother was Educated, Modern, and Telling Me. But telling me what?

It was about periods, that's all, she says, shaking with laughter. You were too young for the details, so I used a metaphor.

'A simile, you mean.'

Oh, you're just like your father, she says, then frowns, remembering.

'No, I was just like you, inside, and you jolly well ought to have explained it better.'

She is frowning. You wait until it's your turn, she says.

'Fair enough.'

All that humanity, love, knowledge, education, womanhood and three generations of females and we couldn't communicate. It fills me with sadness. I shall do better, I swear I will. Oh, let me have ten daughters that I may draw them diagrams.

I must be fair, completely fair. There were times when she was a competent and loving mother.

'I was grateful at the time, though.'

We were camping somewhere again, she says.

'In Wales with those American children who had been our neighbours on the Riviera, and who had been dumped with us so that their mother could have her fifth honeymoon, wasn't it?'

That woman! She laughs. She tries very hard to say 'millionairess' with a mixture of awe and ridicule.

* * *

It was that sort of rain you only get in Wales, where you wonder whether you might drown if you stand in one place for too long. And it started. I had to get her attention away from the ever-demanding American twosome (their jeans *must* be washed daily) and confer privately with her inside the tent. She had everything ready and explained all the complications of elastic belts, loops, pads and so on. There was only one toilet on the campsite which was working, and a queue, despite the rain, about half a mile long. I waited in that queue with my equipment under my mac for what seemed hours, only able vaguely to guess at the devastation that was going on below.

'I had to queue for the little hut, a leaking wooden shed with no light. And in my anxiety to do it all right the first time, and because of the restricted place and unfamiliar operations, I dropped the sanitary towel down the toilet.'

My mother is now shaking and shrieking with laughter, remembering. I rub her back, lean her upright again, so that she might restore herself to equilibrium soon, and remind her of the sleeping condition of the rest of the passengers.

The Trained One does a brief tour of inspection, smiles at us as she passes. My mother stops laughing for a moment and then turns to me and bursts out again.

'I *thought* you'd be furious. I stood there, watching it grow and swell in the water at the bottom of the pan and burst into tears. But there were half a million people waiting to use the hut. You weren't cross, though; you laughed and said "that's Sod's Law" and gave me two more and I queued again. You just laughed.'

Thank you for getting it right. Thank you.

How she laughs! Nothing pleases my mother like poor taste humour, the slightly seedy.

The pilot passes again, followed by the Trained One, guiding him gently. I had forgotten he was there. He turns and gives us a brief smile and staggers on down the aisle. He returns shortly, however, with more tools, a broader grin and no Trained One.

What above earth's going on?

'It was always winter in Lewisham. Always Christmas.'

She laughs. It can't have been, she says.

'No, it's true. I bet if we landed there now, it would be early Christmas morning.'

As the rain turned into frost and crisped Blackheath, the connection between school and home faded completely: at school we heard of the Immaculate Conception and questioned the cook who agreed that it was not possible, looking over her shoulder at the stairs up to the rest of the school, a large Victorian house, and towards the apartments of the headmistress who would doubtless excommunicate her on the spot for such utterances. At home Nanny prepared for a siege, getting in the ingredients for the Pagan Feast to which all relatives this side of the Atlantic would come.

From time to time she would expire and sit in the Alcove, a small padded recess where she was safe from the loving attentions of Tommy and the endless questions we put to her about the Universe, the Immaculate Conception and the Traction Engine. My mother would hobble in from work with her stick and make sarcastic comments about how difficult it must be for her doing the odd bit of housework and trying not to overtax herself.

'Even Grandpa Wells came.'

All the relatives, braving the fog and snow to come and stay. I'm not having *him* here, she used to say, he's a dirty old man, covered in ash, and he never remembers to bring the children presents.

We only had to have him the once, she says.

The two extremes of the family: Nanny with her superstition, proverbs, practical lovingkindness based on an oversimplified misunderstanding of Christianity, and Grandpa Wells: a fiercely intellectual Militant Atheist.

So we'd all be there, before he came, around the

90

kitchen table in the steamy kitchen in darkest London, a tribe with its own rituals and Nanny would say, 'Well, lovies, here we all are, together, excepting those of us across the Atlantic.' The Atlantic, as if it were the Styx. Not quite, my mother would say, I'm sorry to say my husband has invited his father. My father never made the eloquent defence of his father which I expected. He had only to remind my mother that it was his father who had given them the deposit for the house. Given. And she was subdued into sulky agreement.

Gloria would say that the sins of the father were not visited upon the son necessarily, and Arnold would interrupt, apologize, and say that he was sure there was no-one should be turned away at this particular time of the year, and we ought to search our hearts for the Seasonal Spirit, always being careful not to mention any specific theologies, for fear of being found unnacceptable himself, cast as he was each year among the Pagan at the time of Christ. The Pagan being my father and his father, and, increasingly, me.

But you could feel the chill of Catholicism dripping down from the cracked ceiling with his every breath.

We would drink port and wait for the arrival. In the front room with the long theatrical moth-eaten curtains, we waited. Odd jokes pierced the smoky air, always the same, ritual jokes. My father would remark, kindly, that Nanny was five feet three inches *short* not five feet three inches *tall*. Perhaps he won't come. We fiddled idly with the harmonica, ukulele, piano, violin.

And waited. Waited for the curtain to go up, so to speak. Waited, knowing that my mother didn't want him, her mother didn't want him, her brother-in-law found him blasphemous and her sister, scandalous.

Tommy and I were more self-interested: either he brought no presents, or he gave out five-pound notes from his waistcoat pocket; you never knew what to expect. It lent a sense of adventure to Christmas.

When he arrived, with a mere knock on the door, like other mortals, his presence was felt throughout the

91

house as a ripple, like some inexpressible change in the weather, rather than the simple addition of one. He would stand in the hallway and the hall seemed suddenly grand, suddenly gothic. He still had all the majesty of an opera singer, and still the voice. His hair was thick and bristled iron grey; his long eyebrows strained to meet it, like the two pointed ears of a polecat. His nose sprouted a cluster of tobacco-stained blond hairs, and when he bent to kiss me the smell of ash was enough to take my breath away.

That terrible man, my mother is tsking, even now.

How could I know, at my age? Or Tommy, at his?

'I remember Uncle spilt some port on his trousers and Grandpa said, "Rejoice, Arnold, for a port on the trousers is worth two in the tummy!" He was always amusing us.'

She didn't laugh, she says.

Perhaps he was the only one who met those Midas eyes and out-stared them? Perhaps he upstaged her too successfully?

'I suppose the Atheism was a bit much at Christmas?'

Not just agnosticism, but strident and eloquent atheism. All things were conceptual: nothing was simply itself. There were not *real* or *artificial* Christmas trees, he informed Tommy and me, for all trees wrenched out of the ground where they belonged, and brought indoors and got up like fairgrounds were artificial by definition. Presents were a substitute for love; there was no Father Christmas, no Jesus, only the generosity of parents trying to prove something. He was Anarchy on fire with volcanic ash which accumulated with every thought he formed and puffed out towards the heavens, which were only and always just the galaxies, planets and stars. Mumbo-jumbo: polished comforts for a forgotten world.

I could not understand then why my mother hated him so, for he seemed a glorious being to me, and at the same time, a loving grandfather. But what was

92

overwhelmingly obvious was that my father loved him very much. It was enviable, and inexplicable.

Grandpa Wells had not been, after all, a good father in the conventional sense. Indeed he had been, if looked at objectively, a 'bad' father. He had dragged my father, as a small boy, from one pub to the next, playing piano for a precarious living; he had given him so unstable a childhood that the Yorkshire relatives had taken him on from time to time to give him some 'family life'. And I myself saw eventually the one room where they had lived, slept, and where my father had cooked for them when he should have been kicking a ball on the streets outside.

So – love is not a refund. Love is not what you *get back* in return for anything. It is something else. Grandpa Wells was a man of ideas – a Fabian, an Idealist, a gambler on the Stock Market, a Militant Atheist, a great reader. But it was not any of these things that mattered. What did matter? I don't know; but I know that love is not a refund. If I loved my mother, it was not because she was well; neither can you hate someone for being ill.

'I suppose it was Arnold's Christian duty to maintain calm in the face of all his blasphemy?'

Arnold is himself a very great theologian, in a quiet sort of way, I am informed.

'Remember how I would pester Nanny to play the piano for us?' Romantic dance-hall music, 'Autumn Leaves' and 'My Blue Heaven'. I found the sheet music once with 'Wings of a Dove.'

Some song they sang, my mother is trying to remember.

'It was Wings of a Dove.'

Yes.

The room fell into a stiff auditorial silence as she started to tinkle out the notes. Grandpa Wells stood up and approached. He stationed himself by the old upright, his hands clasped before him, as he does on those old photographs from the D'Oyly Carte where he is some King or other, and began.

'Oh, for the wings, for the wings . . .' and appealed to Nanny with his eyes to sing the harmony. Her voice was scratchy at first, but both voices carried and were in tune.

'You must have been taken back, Mummy, you and Gloria, remembering your mother singing to you and Babs on rainswept winter afternoons in Blackheath, all those years ago.'

I was. I was overwhelmed, though as if with the memory of something which had not yet happened. Disparate, entwined voices at the extremes of range. The music swelled and tapered. I was spellbound. All the more poignant was this as they were both aware, I am sure, that they had absolutely no other means of communicating. This was a transient and artificial cooperation, but oh, the result was sweet and mysterious. We were like a happy family then, or rather, like a family caught off-guard between tragedies.

'An almost perfect moment.'

Why do you say *almost*? she was bound to ask.

'Well, you didn't want him there!'

A few weeks later, struggling with my new paint-by-numbers or a spirograph, downstairs on the kitchen table, I heard the phone ring along the corridor and then a cry and something banging the wall. It was the news that Grandpa Wells had fallen from the window of the nursing home and had not survived the fall.

I watched the blond hairs in my father's nose as he told us; they wavered, in and out. 'How could he fall from a window?' 'We don't need to know that. It makes no difference.'

It appears they had trimmed the other nose-hairs when they applied the heavy theatrical make-up which was still fashionable for corpses in those days, because he had none.

He was in costume for his final performance: the flame-dance with no return, performed without benefit

94

of nets, company, or breath. The pay-off, his wings, his dove-wings.

But that was not the music over the speakers in the Crematorium: it was a dreadful medley of hymns so horrible it is a wonder Grandpa did not rise out of his coffin to denounce their Poor Taste, and refuse to be cremated to mumbo-jumbo music.

During the funeral and in cars before and afterwards, old old uncles I had never met conversed freely, jovially.

– What odds d'ye gie y'sen?

– A fiver, me afore you.

– Dead men make bad debtors.

– The money willed Oxfam, either way.

– Done.

I couldn't believe it. My father smiled; he liked it. Had I misunderstood, then? Oh, Death, where is thy turf-accountant?

It was alright, really it was.

We came back to London and the very traffic seemed a comfort, and a welcome. At school Harriet asked me if I had had a good funeral, and then said, sorry, you don't say that, do you?

The trains at the end of the garden continued to pass: rickety-rack, rickety-rack.

That night, I couldn't sleep, thinking about him. Perhaps I was too young for a funeral. There was a faint light under their door.

'One night, seeing the light under your door, I came in to ask about Grandpa. I didn't know what I wanted to ask, only that I wanted to ask it so badly.'

A rhythmic choking sound was coming from the bed, from my father's side.

'Tell me where Grandpa has gone. Tell me the truth, I said. Imagine! Tell me the Meaning of Life, quick, now. Just like children, isn't it, Mum: tell me a simple thing quickly – I don't want all that explanation, just the Answer.'

I wish I knew, was all he said. I wish I knew.

* * *

And on the other side, the far side of their bed, her eyes. Her dry eyes. This is where it gets you, all that intellect, all that education. Nowhere. Only confusion awaits you. Let *him* suffer for a change; don't I suffer always?

– Mummy!

– Go to bed now.

Keep out. There are no dogs, no night terrors, no palliatives, no afterlife, no need of comfort. There is no comfort in me for you.

On my way back I check Tommy's breathing. He is still alive, and so is the cat on the end of his bed. And so are the fleas in her coat, though I have no way of checking. And the micro-organisms on the backs of the fleas in her coat . . .

Lying down, I check the postage stamps are in place under my nightdress and drift, trying to concentrate on infinity. The grown-up world had betrayed me and the stars were only and always from then on, just the stars.

9 Road Finish

The past, too, is slipping away, through my fingers, up out into the starry dark.

The lights in the toilets go on. The captain, no soberer, but triumphant, swaggers past us and speaks jovially with the gay steward in the circle of light cast in the galley on the wings.

My mother seems to be asleep. So I say, softly, hoping against hope:

'Not sleeping, are you?'

No, she is not, she is resting her eyes and she hopes it is alright to rest them occasionally, that I don't *mind*.

'Yes, that's alright. Of course.'

She is implying something else, but I am too weary now to imagine what. It is hard enough to keep a distinct grip on the past.

'You marched into my bedroom in Lewisham, the first floor one, not the attic one, where I and my mumps were watching Robin Hood on a television specially installed for the occasion, and asked me if I'd like to go to Africa on a ship.'

It was one of those questions which are in essence rhetorical. More of a command than an enquiry. But put in the form of a question in order to astound the more.

Oh, I can decide, can I, on such a massive issue?

Amazing.

All the more so because I was ill, and so more completely than usual under her absolute power. And how she relished that absolute power! She was suddenly a caryatid of efficiency: the sheets were whisked off and renewed with a Houdini sleight-of-hand, while you pretended to sleep. There was no need; I could have got out of bed and stood by while she changed the sheets. But it was more impressive that way. Just lie there, Jane, I'm just – whisk – there – all done. Keep your tongue still, and on *top* of the thermometer. The doctor had been, had been humoured a little, and allowed to prescribe an antibiotic for the complications I was suffering which she had pointed out to him, to save his actually needing to examine me. He was a 'sweet' man, but rather old-fashioned, she said, giving me *two* teaspoonfuls of antibiotic, to get levels high in the bloodstream quicker. But it says on the bottle . . . never mind that, who knows best?

You, Mummy. Always.

My father too was only tolerated with an amused sort of patience like a rather tiresome visitor to the ward. Your father has just popped in to say Hello. Hello Dad. There, don't tire her out now; off you go.

Lovely juicy mumps – so big I couldn't move my head. Such food for conversation afterwards – of course the virus had a field-day – all abdominal glands affected, the lot; but I kept her out of hospital.

No, Nanny, a mustard poultice would *not* help. Just go and make the dinner for the others, will you?

Would you like to go to Africa?

Well . . .

That's how I remember it. As if I rose up out of my sickbed (anything's better than mumps . . .) and up the gangplank of an Elder Dempster passenger liner bound for the West Coast of Africa. There must have been weeks of preparation and packing, though she always was the world's fastest packer. I used to think, when I read about Jews having to leave their homes in the dead of night to escape the Nazis, that my mother would have managed the essential packing even under those circumstances. She was at her best when packing,

98

especially with insufficient time and a patient in the background.

'You finally taught me to swim. On that ship.'

Her 'resting' eyes open at this and she makes a motion to rub them, misses, and I duck to avoid the wide arc of the barbed wire.

'Sink or swim method.'

It was; for the surging tilt of the ship made first a shallow pond of the part I was standing in, and then a fathom-deep. I had to swim uphill and down. She stood or sat at the side, exhibiting uncharacteristic patience, shouting encouragement and instructions to me. No one else would come in; it was too rough. The concentration involved was intense: I thought no more about why my parents were always arguing, when Nanny would join us, and whether there were unimaginable spiders everywhere in Africa.

I stopped drowning and started swimming. No-one ever forgets the moment. As we rounded the West Coast, the weather calmed, the sea calmed, the air warmed up, and the pool, my pool, was invaded.

Germans, French, Spaniards and even Americans fell into the pool and pushed one another under. The crew organised greasy pole competitions over it, fancy dress parties in it and on the whole it was not possible to do three consecutive strokes anywhere, even of dog-paddle.

– Come in, Mum! Why don't you come in? She only need to have shouted back that she didn't want to, or couldn't swim properly any more, but instead she made grotesque faces at me and mouthed the words 'I can't'. Why not? I shouted back, naturally enough. She stormed away, leaving me to the mercies of splashing teenagers and a guilty conscience about whatever it was I had done to offend her.

I drip, towelless, back into the ship. The walls of the corridors are the same studded hot tin down here as they are in our bedrooms, *staterooms*. There are lips at every threshhold. Heavy firedoors divide the ship into incomprehensible portions. Drip-drip. People turn and stare at me, making my way back down to the cabin.

It's the tropics, people kept saying, it's the tropics: headaches, depressions, seasickness, poor meals, boredom, rashes. It's just the tropics, you can rely on it. No-one is here on a cruise: they are all going somewhere for a purpose. Trunks full of effects in the hold, two more floors below me, dogs exercised in the Special Zone with sand for the doggy dos on the far end of the Officers' Deck, two floors up.

Nearly there. The temperature, which has risen and risen recently, beyond what seemed to be the ultimate extent of heat, rises as I penetrate the ship. Down here plastic beach shoes would melt. The soles of my feet are warm and dry already.

'Remember how the heat affected people. Their small talk shrivelled up and disappeared. We had to play cards and Scrabble in the shade of the Games Room, near the fans, rather than be outside.' Quinine daily, and codeine for headaches, drugged and dizzy.

Over the lip into the airlocked metal-walled room and up to the top bunk. Tommy is having his nap on the bottom one. I sink, wet, into the bedding. My ear pressed against the hot tin wall, I can hear them next door.

– You don't always have to take her side. It's not obligatory.

– What *sides*? Is there a war?

– You know very well what I mean and what I have to put up with. Battles, battles. I'm criticized all the time, but when your precious daughter. . .

– Oh, come on Charlie, don't exaggerate!

– She's just a child, you don't seem to realize.

– Then forget it. Put it down to inexperience.

– She did it deliberately.

– Why would she do that?

– To *humiliate* me.

– How can you say that? Think that?

– For God's sake, she's not a child any more!

100

– You just said she was.

– Is this an interrogation? I'm not one of your little students. Or had you forgotten? I'm your wife.

– How could I forget?

– What did you say?

– Nothing.

– You did *not* say nothing. People don't inspirate, brace their diaphragms and release air between the chords of the larynx and produce *nothing*.

– And what does all that signify?

– That you're a *liar*.

Doors open, shut. The room lurches and I am thrown from the wall to the rail of the bed.

– Jane, your mother would like. She feels. If you could try to be more sensitive.

– Yes, I know.

– Do you?

– Course.

– Fine. Good girl. Better change. You're all wet.

– Yes. I know.

I feel so ill all the time. Dare I complain about it? What régime might come into effect, should I dare to say?

– Mummy, I don't feel very well.

– None of us do: it's the heat. Try not to think about the heat for, say, one minute.

Futile. It cannot be done. Like trying not to think about sand in the Sahara.

Then you must get exercise, all of you. A person could atrophy and become an invalid unless they walk once round the entire ship three times a day.

Tommy and I tour the decks of sweating, dying grown-ups laid out on wooden beds along the inner edge of the deck for their siesta, speculating on the fate of those doggy-dos on the Officers' Deck. Tommy wants to liberate one of the scrappy little animals, flopping about in the heat, which we can just see by standing on the second step of the flight with 'No Entry First Class Only' over it. Difficult, because I have to hold his hand at all times as I have been warned that should he slip under the bottom railing at the edge of the ship, he would certainly drown and it would be my fault. There would be no stitching him up in hospital – he would be gone forever.

– What would you do with it, if you had it?

– Play with it, course.

– Maybe we can have a pet when we get to Africa.

– They don't got pets in Africa; it's jungle.

It was not difficult to keep him away from the rail at the edge of the deck: Tommy was terrified at the expanse of water around us in any case, for his own reasons.

'And you kept telling me, people pay money for this, they actually chose to spend weeks on a ship as a holiday.'

Fly too, she says, looking down the aisle. Some of these people are going on holiday.

'It's not the same; it's not like a prison sentence, a few hours on a plane.'

Oh, I don't know, she says, with a twist in her voice.

I laugh.

'It's not *that* bad, is it?'

With a violent paroxysm she shifts away from me and cranes her neck back. How can anyone *know* how bad it is for her? she asks, tears in her eyes.

'I'm sorry. I shouldn't have said that. Only if anyone can make a good guess, it's me.'

And that's all anyone can hope for isn't it? An educated guess or two – about how other people feel, about how the world works? We are all guessing.

I had seen no documentaries about Nigeria, read no novels set there, nor seen posters of children with distended bellies on the walls of Oxfam shops. Africa was stranger to me then than it would be to anyone now.

But on the other hand I had quite a different notion of black people from most children of my age and nationality. There had always been a high proportion of black people at those parties, at dinner as guests, as strangers asleep on the studio couch in the morning. And they had all been princes, Doctors of Philosophy, representatives of some exotic government overseas. This gave me the impression that all black people were intellectual, articulate, exotic, friendly and fairly wealthy. Hence when we arrived at a country where almost everyone was black, it seemed to me that we were somewhere fantastic, the homeland of that species of specially talented people I had come to regard as my father's superiors, as his 'bosses' even.

My mother had none of these advantages, and found it more difficult to adjust. She was forever pointing out the swollen bellies of infants by the roadside with horror and disgust: these people ought to know how to look after their own children at least. I assumed these children were malnourished because of something the rest of the world was responsible for. The idea must have been put to me.

Tommy had an even greater advantage: no preconceptions whatsoever. After a few weeks of playing with black toddlers, he was asking what was wrong with his skin. Why had it not turned black yet? Some people are white and some are brown, some pink . . . that's all. Then I'll be black. No, you can't. He covered his entire body with black shoe-polish the next day, and was streaked and mottled for weeks afterwards.

So, the same journey can give rise to different destinations: my parents had arrived at different places. My mother had come to alien territory, out of date, threatening, anarchic; my father found himself in the actualization of a theory – the humorous well-meaning, traditional world he had written about but never seen. Knowing this, he could defer to men whom my mother knew were about to cheat him. And they did. But my father's astonishment at their villainy was never diminished; often exasperated, he never joined the

103

conspiracy. He made appeals to the honesty of the most shifty characters, and, sometimes, to the astonishment of everyone concerned, just in a blue moon, obtained it.

No sooner had we arrived than a small aircraft and a taxi were needed. There was a whole dockside conference on the topic. My mother was terrified, hysterically describing the vehicle as 'nothing but rubber bands operated by a moron'.

This and other journeys on this subcontinent provided me with evidence that there was a limit to my father's patience – and the parameter was racism. For this, and this alone, he would risk marital fallout. For once returning the Midas Eyes, something of Grandpa Wells's theatricality in his own, he turned to her as the engine juddered and skipped and dipped over the rain forest and said, 'Shut up woman!'

'Remember that awful journey inland from Lagos to Nsukka?'

She does. How could she forget? She is regaining what composure she normally has. It is best to carry on. I can see that.

The taxi ride was, if possible, worse. Hotter for a start. Everyone gathered at the side of the road to stare at us as we passed. The children came in twenties, minimum, and straggled across the red-dust roads shouting 'Onyatcha!' (white men) at us.

My father rolled down his window and shouted 'Onyatchi!' (black men). They were amazed and amused.

My mother warned my father that should he open his window and let the insects in one more time she would return to England on the next boat.

Further and further into the interior we seemed to travel, through acres of palm trees, ground-nut, cola nut, miles of potholes. To the campus of Nsukka University, incongruously designed on the American Land Grant model.

'Best colonial style à la 1963 with, even I have to admit, bungalows. Bungalows with verandahs and with or without gardens, to suit both English and American colonials.'

We stood, dazed, on 'our' street, a rough red dirt avenue approximating the European idea of a street, when the most enormous person I had ever seen rose up in front of us.

'Remember Gabriella?'

Many things are overblown on the Equator: leaves, fruit, young girls, roses, tempers; but of them all, Mrs Professor Gabriella Alcock-Smythe was the most spectacular. Her sense of her own importance was the only thing on earth which rivalled the enormity of her appearance.

She was over six feet tall, about twenty stone (due to thyroid malfunction and her own greed in equal proportions, according to the expert on Matters Medical) and her ebony skin was swathed with yards and yards of blue material, some of which was intricately wound around her head to rise a further foot into the sky. And swaying about her like a timid pet, was a two-foot long feather fan, held together with embroidered leather thongs.

It was Gabriella who had engaged our servants, Gabriella who had ordered our first meal, chosen our furniture out of Campus Stores, Gabriella who warned us about snakes and spiders, malicious gossip about herself, putting too much trust in the servants she had engaged for us. Finally, it was Gabriella who enquired what arrangements were being made to ensure the safe arrival of the grandmother she had 'heard' was travelling by aeroplane?

For Nanny had wisely avoided the 'cruise' but was needed to assist my mother. At least, that had been the idea, but it became apparent during Gabriella's opening remarks, during which, as if in response to some invisible cue, several black people, servants, had emerged from behind our bungalow to greet us, that we would not be 'needing' this assistance.

Mummy held her fire on Gabriella. It was shrewd so to do. You could have fitted two of my mother in Gabriella's powerful right arm. I could see she was only wondering how to befriend her without losing face. Some instinct told you that to cross swords with Gabriella was to court disaster, even death.

Nanny wasn't as out of place as I had foreseen: she hadn't been born in India for nothing, she declared.

But she *was* out of place in the kitchen, now Tobias's kitchen. She would stand, watching him do some operation a strange way, longing to give him some advice, but afraid of offending him. He would catch her watching, stop what he was doing and freeze. Did madam need something from his kitchen? No, no, you carry on. And she would leave. Not thrown out, just frozen out.

    – What do you want me to do, Charlie?
    – Nothing. What do you think we pay the servants for?
    – Couldn't I do something they can't do for you? I could make Jane a party dress from that material . . .
    – Why? There aren't any parties.
    – Or these sofa cushions; everyone has blue! I could . . .
    – They belong to Campus Stores. What would be the point? I think she may have been set the task of teaching Tommy to read. But he could so easily side-track her, had so much else to say (of greater interest anyway, Nanny would agree), and in any case Nanny obviously did not really approve of so young a child being 'overstimulated'.
    – In any case, Charlie, I'm a musician, not a teacher.
    – A *what*?
Howls of laughter, absolute howls.
    A woman came and made wallcharts and taught Tommy to read in a fortnight. She attacked the business

like an army officer, marching little Tommy into his room for one hour each day, with a pile of charts and books, and would 'brook no interruption'. When she had taught him to read, she quit. Job done. Payment made. Like someone employed to fumigate the basement, or lop trees.

– I'll mind the children, Charlie. You go out and enjoy yourself. Go shopping, anything.

– My driving is dodgy now, and Tobias has done all the shopping, and the children no longer need 'minding'.

It was true. I was old enough to ride my old Raleigh around the streets of the campus, the potholes making a slalom course. There were no gaps for her to fill, outwardly. There was no *excuse* for her; she was just there. And thank God, I said, daily.

Everyone is something, says Tobias: small boy, gardener, under-gardener, general man, or cook. You have only to shout towards the servants' quarters, which are simply whitewashed huts with corrugated tin roofs, hugging the rear fence, with only a standing pipe for plumbing, where Tobias' barren wife, their adopted child, his other wife, their cousins, and their children and their teenage cousins all live, cook, sleep and sing. Only I can't. I can't yell for a grown-up. I slink down the garden to their place and, as I approach, the children run indoors as if from danger, and Mrs Tobias the First comes and frowns at me a moment before she curtseys. Oh please don't; how I loathe it.

– Ask your mother if there's anything she wants, Jane.

– What's that whispering in there? Nan!

Nanny winces. She pulls a face. I know what she is thinking. It is an insult, to call her Nan, rather than Mum. Gloria and Babs call her Mum; but they haven't any children says my mother, that's why.

– Nothing Charlie. I was just wondering if there is anything you want doing.

– You could better yourself, Nan.

– How's that?

– You could learn Efik from the servants.

Nanny settles herself opposite on an armchair and picks up her knitting. Knitting! The thought of wool makes you feel ill. I can only vaguely remember vests let alone pullovers.

– I think I'm too old for that sort of caper. You can't teach an old dog. I found French hard enough at school. Mercy buckets pardonnay mwa and all that.

– Sounds like reasonable Efik, doesn't it Jane?

– She's only joking, Mum.

– She's not. Swiss finishing: they finished off your Nan good and proper there!

Pearl one, knit one, pearl two, knit one. Click. Click.

– Your mother left school at fourteen, Jane, I'll have you know.

– Fourteen!

– They only taught us how to pick raspberries, nothing else.

– Your mother is exaggerating. Quite a wild one, your Mum.

She glances up from the knitting, upways over the moons of her bifocals.

– She's confused. She's thinking of Babs. She means your Aunty Babs.

– *She* is the cat's mother.

My mother sighs, melodramatically.

– What was *that* in aid of?

– Sudden increase in the need for oxygen. The hypothalamus is very sensitive.

Matters Medical; battle over, and won.

'Once the car came, our new one, we travelled around a lot.'

Tobias, the cook, being promoted to Interpreter when it was discovered by chance that he spoke several languages fluently. He was embarrassed, during these long journeys through the jungle in all directions, that my father sat him in the front passenger seat while my mother had to sit in the back with the children. Of course it was supposed to be for ease of communication, so that he could easily roll down the window and ask for directions, suggest bribes, request removal of a goat (child, hut, truck) from the road, or even jump out to discuss things with roadside tradesmen. But he was still the servant riding as it were *in precedence* over the mistress. I often wondered if he wasn't in fact better company for my father not only because he had an almost inexhaustible fund of folklore and anecdote to tell about the areas we travelled through, but also because since my father was to him a minor deity, he never criticized him in any way. It must have been a sort of emotional holiday, having him as co-pilot.

'Our first ever entirely new car – the Ford Zephyr.'

Oh, it was a *lovely* car, she says.

When Tommy and I, later, in the cruel and witty phase of our adolescences, wished to mimic my mother, we always put 'lovely' every third word.

All the servants had stood around the shining new car, saying 'our motor, our motor' with fervour and love. But my father's pleasure, delayed by weeks and weeks, as he had waited for it to be shipped out, was tempered by the mysterious fact that it had many thousands of miles on the clock already. The man who delivered it so late had been using it as a taxi in Lagos. It was only due recompense, all the servants agreed, for the man's trouble in delivering it so far from the capital. All the servants were prepared to tolerate it; my father sighed, shook his head, lit his pipe, and prepared himself to tolerate it.

But my mother could not tolerate it. She could not abide slackness. The man should be reported; otherwise my father's goodwill would be taken advantage of again.

'Travelling, interviewing, travelling.'

It had always been my father's ambition, a Boys' Own desire, to sail down the Niger. So much mystery and romance surrounded this desire of his that I thought the Niger was an Amazon, and we to discover its source.

A long journey we had into the interior, having left Tobias in Calabar to visit his other two thousand relatives.

'Road Finish'.

Just a sign and a village by the side of a puddle several hundred yards across.

– We can't go any further, dear; this is it.

– Don't be ridiculous! Get twenty black men to carry the car over.

– What?

– You heard me; there are hundreds of them just loafing about there. Get them to pick up the car and *walk across*. You can give them a penny each.

– You must be joking. She is joking, isn't she, Jane?

– I don't think so.

– Bloody Hell.

The head man came across, six youths flanking him. There were greetings exchanged. My father enquired after his mother and her relatives, his crop, his goats. They were just getting to the subject of the flood over the road when my mother interrupted with a stream of invective to the effect that she could wait no longer and would shortly wade into the lake herself.

My father shuffled the group further off and pointed in the direction of the water. I could no longer hear what they were saying but the headman came back to my mother's open window and said,

– Water him not very tall, Madam. You gowan drive him good good.

– Won't the car sink then?

– Yes.

– What?

– Yes, it won't.

Stupid, stupid, mutters my mother under her breath.

I have to speculate (in answer to her repeated questions) on what the Hell my father might think he is up to now. Well, I know what it is – there is more talk needed. Nothing must be done abruptly, it is bad manners.

Perhaps the professor's family would like to share in a

cola nut with the headman and his wives? Perhaps a bargain might be struck whereby my father would exchange me for several very very good zebu cows and four goats?

By the time we drove through the short water, wetting our brakes terminally, even my mother had to laugh. My father assured us that the offer was staggeringly generous and simply meant as a compliment.

All the way down the Niger, the boat sitting so low in the red-brown water that water-skimming insects looked us in the eye, I tried to imagine being the twentieth wife of that old black man, living the rest of my life out by the not very tall puddle under the Road Finish sign.

And the next time my parents were not speaking to each other, I thought there might be something to be said for it.

To Aba, Port Harcourt, Benin City, Ibadan, Kano and Kaduna. Stopped on a plain somewhere while my father consults the map. A man passes on a horse and he and my father fail to make meaningful contact. They have no common language. Great, says my mother – we are lost in Africa, you can't speak the language and we've left Tobias in Calabar. Great.

There is no need to be melodramatic, it is not my father's fault. Imagine, if you will, that some ninny from the Colonial Office one day drew a line from Chelmsford to Gloucester and said, these are two countries from now on. No-one would really mind very much, would they?

The North and the South – okay, we can live with it. But supposing he drew it from Portsmouth to Newcastle and said these are two countries. What then? That would be ridiculous. In fact, there might be civil war. Well, said my father, that is what we did to Nigeria. We said, let's draw a square boundary here and here and here and here and call it Nigeria, because the River Niger flows through it.

111

This eloquence did nothing to mollify my mother.

– We shall stay at the first Rest House we come to, and to Hell with finding Kano.

The next morning my father walked out of the storm-doors of our chalet and a mile down the road for a newspaper. We went to have breakfast, paw-paw with limes, on the verandah of the dining hut. He came back through the net doors, still speckled with the cloggings of the night's insects, and said 'Kennedy's been shot dead'. Of course this now mighty commonplace was happening the world over at roughly that very moment, making allowances for the time zones, but he said it in the middle of Nigeria to a room full of Americans, and every single one of them burst out crying and wept openly, and the hotel staff, perhaps fearing that the world was about to come to an end, took cover. At last I realized that Nigeria was on the planet earth.

'Think of it, Mum: ask any American over the age of twenty what they were doing when they heard the news of Kennedy's assassination, and they can tell you down to the last detail. About thirty-five of them will recall *him* walking through those storm-doors with the Lagos paper in his hand, saying, in his English voice, simply "Kennedy's been shot dead".'

She is reacting very strangely to this, trying to get nearer to me and shushing me. There might be Americans here, she is saying.

'So?'

They are still funny about it, as if he was a saint, she says, hush, hush.

She wants to draw it out, keep it dark, have a little secret. A major historical event of the twentieth century and she wants to hush it up.

'Um, where were we?' I say, trying to get her to concentrate. She straightens a little, taking her weight off my shoulder and says that she wants to hear about the parrots, then.

'Ah, yes. It was probably Gabriella who suggested, after a while, that we ought to have those African Greys

112

for pets rather than the succession of geckoes, lizards, rats and cats we seemed to collect, and fail to keep alive.'

Rubbish, she says, it was all her idea.

All her idea. Can that be true? Or is it an addition she has made to memory, a fiction. Why on earth should she want us to have parrots?

10 Parrots

Where is everyone? The staff I mean. How do they know for sure whether all the passengers are still alive? How can they tell? What faith they must have.

Or are they having a rave-up forward in the First Class with the Japanese businessmen? Not the Trained One, of course. But the others? How dare they leave us uninterrupted like this!

'Where do you think they've all gone, Mum?'

To sleep, she says.

'No, I mean the stewardpeople.'

She flexes her hands from claw to star and back again and smiles up at me.

She says she hopes that they are sobering the pilot with something effervescent.

Imagine her trying to say 'effervescent'. Imagine my smugness at getting it first time.

'So, it was your idea, was it?'

Your grandmother was so frightened of all those creatures you and Tommy brought into the house, she says.

Nanny was terrified, it's true, of those beings who expired with varying degrees of drama and tragedy, depending on some unwritten scale of how much love you could invest in insect, amphibian or rodent life, in various unsuitable areas of the house and grounds.

She would jump on to some piece of furniture, should she spot a rhinoceros-beetle making its armoured way across the living-room floor and cry out for Tobias to come and 'remove it, if you please'.

Don't be stupid, my mother would say, it's only one of God's creatures. And what will Tobias think? So she would return sheepishly to her sewing, or knitting, knowing that as soon as my mother was out of sight, Tobias would send the Small Boy to remove the insect, for Tobias was softening towards her. First she was Mrs Madam's mother, then she was The Grandmother, then Our Grandmother and then finally, when she had taught him how to make Dundee cake one afternoon, simply Nah'nee.

You weren't interested in the birds at first, says my mother. She was disappointed because she'd been trying to get them for weeks.

'Yes I remember.'

I was with Megan, a sixteen-year-old English girl from Hampstead who had three younger siblings and a mother who wore Marks and Spencer's night-dresses for sun-dresses. This was spotted by Gabriella who spread it around, adding, 'What a good idea – such an inexpensive way of wearing something no one else is wearing!' When you die, Megan would say, they ought to put your remains on the compost heap to reinvigorate the nitrogen cycle. It's a waste, else. It wasn't their athe-ism which appalled my mother (didn't she live with that day in, day out, anyway?), it was the fact that Megan's mother had produced all four children without the aid of a professional midwife, which was nothing short of scandalous. Four was, in itself, an indication of lack of self-control, unless you were a Catholic.

Megan was showing me a rude book (she was taking a great interest in all things rude that week) under her dining-room table. I don't think I was understanding it but we had only ten minutes before her mother, who had given birth on the teatable (Megan's aunt had cleared it first with one crockery-smashing swish of the table-cloth in a panic and she had lost not only her chocolate cupcake but also the corrugated foil wrapper, unlicked, which was the best bit) which I thought was just about the rudest thing you could imagine, was due to return; so time was precious. Suddenly there was the sound of my mother's voice coming through the mosquito netting on the dining-room window.

– Come quickly, Jane, Megan. See what I've got!

– I don't want to just now; could it wait, Mum?

– No, it bloody well can't wait. What are you doing in there anyway?

And just as we replaced the book on the shelf and scrambled to our feet, she was there, in the room, with the Midas Eyes on full.

On the back seat of the car were my brother Tommy and a nasty tin cage about two foot high. Inside it were the two parrots. I remember saying,

– What is it?

– What do they bloody look like – caterpillars?

Megan and her sister shared a small green monkey who travelled around on their shoulders and peeled its own bananas. We were not to have such a pet because my mother knew exactly what diseases you could get from them.

From these prehistoric things, surely you could catch terminal ugliness?

Their beaks were the size and strength of pliers and were their most prominent feature. Their heads were reptilian, their tongues black and thick, like the moving parts of a snail – and darted about inside their hollow beaks.

Their eyes bulged, swivelling on an axis similar to the frog's. All the feathers were uniformly grey, except for the last two inches at the neat, folded-together tail, where it seemed as if someone had just dipped their rear ends into bright red poster paint. Most prehistoric of all were the talons, every bit as fierce as the eagle's: three long, scaly grey fingers, two at the front and one behind, with claws an inch out, wound around the small wooden perch bisecting the cage.

Pets they might be, but it was hard to imagine loving them, ever.

The parrots were installed in the sitting room, the one with the French windows out to the verandah, on a coffee-table in this pitifully small cage about the size of a modest television set, with a perch and a small swing. Since there was no television, they performed the function of that piece of furniture in more ways than one, though they would not speak. They simply made noises: first the noises of the jungle where they had always lived, of other birds and drums, and then, gradually, the noises near them, such as the sound of the car crunching down the gravel driveway to the French windows.

We argued about whose turn it was to empty the tray at the bottom encrusted with peanut husks, sunflower seeds and droppings, for it was definitely not a servant's job, though the Small Boy, who dreamt of working in a Lagos florist, arranged flowers near the cage to mask the peanut butter smell which exuded constantly from it.

'They spoke first for Gabriella, didn't they?'

Not exactly *for* her, my mother says, grinning.

Gabriella. The shrubs in the front garden would all stiffen, as if in the wake of a juggernaut. Everything is sucked in when Gabriella passes.

– Just have a leetle word with Tobias, Charlotte. With you in a mo-maunt, ma cherie.

She would stand at the door from the dining room into the kitchen rattling away at Tobias in his own language. Tobias stood always on one leg, slanting away from her like the shrubs, answering her obsequiously.

She was not daft. There was not one atom of daft in Gabriella – it was all sheer cunning, all twenty stone of it.

Gabriella comes and sits, flinging aside a wrap – a superfluous four yards of bright blue material – as if to say 'Here, thank God, I can be off my guard', and takes up the whole settee single-bottomed.

– Shall I order some coffee for us? says my mother.

– Taken care of, ma cherie.

She turns to me (creating a draught).

117

– I'm so glad to see Janey wearing shortie shorts. Only the other day I said to myself, soon she will be all grown up and not any longer daring to wear shorts. They are hardly children for one my-*newt* minute are they Charlotte?

– No, indeed, says my mother, her small frame spread as expansively as possible over the armchair, waving her cigarette about like a film star.

– First, says Gabriella, a leetle advice I am needing. You know, Charlotte, that I cannot trust doctors. They are all charlatans, and want only my money.

– Yes.

Gabriella describes some symptoms, something to do with her 'monthlees' or her 'waterworkings'. My mother questions her discreetly and offers advice which Gabriella swears she will take the mo-maunt she gets home because she knows, she says, that my mother's advice is worth its weight in gold since it is based on wide experience in English hospitals.

– I could tell these campus doctors a thing or two, says my mother, laughing.

– I bet you could. Why only the other day, Mrs X, wife of the Professor of . . .

And she imparts some piece of confidential information which she could only possibly have gleaned either by being a fly on the wall of the university medical clinic's consulting room, or by talking with the man who sweeps the floor in the background, invisible to all intents and purposes to the white people who are talking 'in confidence'.

My mother soaks it in, her eyes widening. She encourages Gabriella by inserting, where she falters, the correct medical term.

– Do such things really happen, Mum?

– Oh no, you shouldn't listen to that awful woman, she has no business to spread gossip and rumour like that.

Gabriella pulls a newspaper out from her suitcase of a basket and says,

– Faites attention, as we say in Dahomey, I want you

118

to leesten to this! She reads out an article about an English family in Enugu. The neighbours reported that the children were being badly treated. They were not allowed to behave like children, but were made to do everything for themselves; even the servants were instructed never to help them with anything. After their birthday parties, for instance, there was no way of knowing there had been any festivities, a few hours afterwards. The children had been seen rolling back a carpet, sweeping up mess, whitewashing walls. Wasn't it scandalous, Gabriella wanted to know, that English people could behave like this?

Some people have no idea about children, says my mother. Birth control is now freely available, so why on earth have children if you aren't prepared to put up with some mess from time to time?

Exactly, says Gabriella, drawing out her fan and waving it before her face (creating a hurricane among the ornaments).

Tobias enters with tea: the best set, sandwiches, fruit, and the imported Scottish shortbread kept for royalty. My mother raises her eyebrows to him questioningly but he remains impassive. He does not know before whom to place the tea-tray.

– Who will be mumming him the teapot?

Gabriella has already gone too far ordering the meal in our house, and my mother is not prepared to point it out by saying 'me, of course', so she says,

– Be a dear, Jane.

While I am being a dear, my mother asks Gabriella,

– How old did it say these children were?

– Eleven and thirteen, I think.

My mother takes her tea, spilling it. I fill Gabriella's to the very top, so that she too will spill it, evening the score. She realizes, and stabs me with her eyes.

– Thirteen is almost grown up, says my mother.

– Absoloomaunt!

– In fact, in the old days, a thirteen-year-old often had responsibility for younger siblings.

– Yes, and here we often marry them at that age, if they are mature.

– Children *do* grow up faster.

– Yes.

– Perhaps the mother was, like myself, hard put to move about.

– She may even, ma cherie, be disabled.

– Yes, and then you would expect the children to help a little.

– Yes – just a leetle.

– Have a sandwich, Gabriella. Don't stand on ceremony here.

Gabriella folds forward (creating a tidal wave among the upholstery of the settee) and takes four sandwiches.

– How will they ever learn, continues my mother, any sense of order, if they have only to snap their fingers and a servant comes running?

– You're absolutely right. What is so terreeble about asking a teenager to lend a hand?

– This morning Jane did the ironing, without being asked.

Can you imagine being so bored you did the ironing for fun?

– No, I'm glad you pointed it out, Charlotte, I shall have to read it again; I have miseenterpreted it. I see that now.

Congratulations. You have come full circle from non-sense to nonsense. And when Nanny comes in with Tommy from a walk to the village, they will both fall silent, as if in the presence of inferiors, or servants.

'What was I saying, Mum?'

About the parrots, and Gabriella, says my mother, a musing look creasing her shiny paper-thin skin.

'Ah, yes, we were at the table, having dinner.'

My father was tuning into the BBC World Service in order to puzzle over reports of Beatlemania and topless dresses, at the table, an arch away from the sitting room

120

where the parrots were delicately removing the husks from raw peanuts, under the swish-swishing of the ceiling fan, when Gabriella arrived, unexpectedly, as was her wont.

She came through the French windows.

– Sorry to find you at repast, mes cherries. Please don't disturb yourselves. I shall be quite happy seeting 'ere.

She parked herself on the settee by the coffee-table on which were spread some of my mother's half-read letters.

There was the sound of scurrying and whispering in the kitchen as Tobias let the other servants know who was sitting in the sitting room.

My father continued to fiddle with the radio. We continued to eat, our conversation as constrained by her presence as the servants' movements. She soon became bored and restless and started to leaf through the letters spread out in front of her, and then, quite openly, began reading one which caught her interest.

– What a nerve! said my mother, under her breath. Apparently nobody heard, for my father continued tuning, we eating. The radio whizzed, whistled, and gave out, and in the silence that ensued, one of the parrots called out, unmistakably in my mother's voice:

WHAT A NERVE!

'Of course Gabriella was close to the parrots, so she was bound to hear them. She rose, I remember, like two bison about to charge and stared at us, well at you actually.'

My mother now has her hands over her eyes, tears of silent laughter coursing down her cheeks, shaking with merriment, almost in convulsion. It seemed as if the very ornaments quaked, as if the ebony statues would crack open with stress, under the heat of her anger.

'She, of course, was unaware that by reading your letters she had transgressed any rules of etiquette any more than if she had simply carried on with a jigsaw

121

puzzle left spread out, and she was probably not sure what order of insult "what a nerve" was.'

What else could people expect by leaving letters out for inspection like that? If *she* had left any out they were meant to be read and would be from someone of importance, unlike ours.

Mummy is rocking, gasping, laughing.

'It was no good you denying that you had said it, for the words had your voice-print on them.'

Egging her on to more convulsions.

The bison charged and I can't remember what she actually said, only that it was unspeakable, a brutal mixture of family secrets she could not possibly have known and insinuations, totally unfounded, of racism, snobbery and social ineptitude.

She left, and the letters seemed to want to follow her, in an airborne wake; several objects fell and smashed. Poor Tobias, shaking, on the verge of tears, ran to right the objects and followed her out of the house with an umbrella. It was six o'clock, near the time of the rains, and Mrs Madam herself was not a personage to be let go into the rains without so much as a cup of tea or a Scottish shortbread or ten.

'It was the parrots; they had finally spoken.'

I dry her tears with a tissue: success at last, unmitigated, off-the-graph social disgrace to look back on and laugh about.

'They spoke mostly when people were just around the corner, out of sight, but there. It was always such a surprise when you first heard your phrase parodied so perfectly, every tone correct, and your very own voice, coming from just out of sight, round a corner.'

Chattering, singing, reciting, carrying on conversations in Tommy-voices, me-voices, parent-voices, imitating the kettle, the car, the broom brushing the verandah. They meeowed and whistled, chinked coins, flicked switches, whispered, rang phones near and far, and did the World

Service signature tune over and over again, always preceded by the whirr and squeak of the tuning-in. And as a reward, they won our love. We spoke to them, stroked them, let them out for a 'play', differentiated them, moved their cage into and out of the sun, and named them George and Sam.

She is far away now, far away.

'What are you thinking, Mum?' Penny for your thoughts, as Nanny would say.

We recorded them on the reel-to-reel and they were terrified to hear themselves: they knew it wasn't us teaching them, but their own voices, and they had no voices of their own.

And she now has no voice in the audible world, but a voice of sorts for me.

– Penny for your thoughts, Nan.

– I shall be leaving soon.

– You mean going home? To England? All night long it seemed, I had heard raised voices, angry voices, of the three of them, and shapes had moved to and fro, dark against the pale grey of the mosquito netting. My parents did not argue awkwardly like people unaccustomed to their darker sides. Their eloquence outstripped every threshold and carried on through the border into the no man's land of pure rage.

In the morning, no-one had words left; they were all argued out, and something had changed.

– Do you want to go, Nan?

– In a way, yes. In a way.

There ought to be musak on aeroplanes. The silence is eerie. Lifts always have music floating in them. It makes the weightlessness bearable. The tottering brain can hang on to the odd phrase or pattern of notes. Always weak music; weak, violin versions of 'Penny Lane' or 'Eleanor Rigby'. The past: just a thin floating in the top of the aeroplane, a whisper, a tune. It would be good to have a thinner version of the World Service signature

123

tune to hang on to, over the Atlantic on a dark August night, with the pilot incapable.

After Nanny had gone, the Harmattan came and red dust hung in the air and entered the lungs. Megan and I were restless and rode our bikes around the dry, empty campus at noon, when the whole place had settled down for siesta. We tried to play tennis and failed. Faint and sunstruck, we would seek shade and invent stories about the young VSOs who taught us Latin and Biology.

'Good times, eh? Remember my first driving lesson on that rough track around the campus? The youngest driver in the world?'

Just in case, she said. We all knew that she was ill, but we didn't mention it. The undertow to everything, even this.

My father would say I was too young, it was against the law, except on private roads, and that would be that – that is the assumption between us. In fact, he would not. What he would say is that should any such emergency occur, whereby my mother should be unable to carry on driving somewhere, I should run for help, rather than covering up the problem by driving home for her.

So, let us conspire together, she means, us women. She is, I know only too well, a volatile ally (hasn't even Gabriella turned enemy on her?) and in any case, ally against whom? I don't want to conspire against my father: I have no cause, no desire to. And yet I want to drive – badly. She knows that and, ruthless as Gabriella drawing up Convocation High Table invitations, uses it.

I became quite proficient after three lessons. Probably most twelve-year-olds would; you just have no sense of the enormity of the risk at that age, no sense at all.

You were a good little driver, she says.

'And that time there was the plane strike and he was stuck up North?'

He had gone to the North, to Kano, on business and he

couldn't get home. For six days we heard nothing. Tobias consoled my mother, though he too had tears standing always in his eyes, and he too scanned the windows on the hour, with the fact that six days late in Nigeria is not the same as six days late in England: time is different.

When he did get back, he was in a battered old taxi with five black men who wanted beer and too much money, which they claimed they had been promised. Tobias wanted to run them out of the house with machetes, largely, it seemed, because of their tribal affiliations, but the atmosphere suggested, as they all trooped in, that my father would somehow not be alive if it were not for them.

It wasn't just their colour or their tribe; they were not the same sort of men as my father, not the same sort of men as our servants, our extended household. My father had fallen among bad company. They wore European dress, tight trousers, loud ill-fitting shirts; they were bulbous, breathy, sweaty. Glittering silver beads of sweat stood on the black lurex of their violent faces. As testament to the sense of danger they presented, Tobias and his large cousin, Eme, would not leave the room until they did and crouched, as they never had before and never did since, in the corner of the room, like body-guards prepared to spring.

These were people on the other side of all my father's principles, whatever they were. He was on a sharp edge of offending them. Perhaps he had been put in a position where he had been obliged to be dishonest, to save his life. Had not six days elapsed? What had he had to do or see done? He had travelled for six days without sleep. His eyes were pale and staring. He was like a man who has been tortured and is not sure whether he survived it or not, whether he 'broke' or was spared.

I was so worried, she says, choking a little, even now.

I want to say, that's good then, to remember loving him so much, and fearing he was dead. But I can't say this. There is too much pain in her wringing hands and I am on the borders of sympathy, which is dangerous. For it is only too easy at this moment to imagine myself waiting for my husband for six days without news, to imagine the despair.

'You used to give your cast-offs to Tobias's main wife. Remember how we'd peek out at her parading for the relatives in the latest dress, without shoes or stockings, down their end of the garden?'

My mother had hundreds of these dresses, all drip-dry, all shirtwaisters, all the same length (just covering the knee). Only the colour varied, but whatever colour, it was the wrong colour for black skin – navy, plum.

The dignity of the tall woman in the Marks and Spencer's dress was always remarkable; never did Gabriella in all her glory appear like this. Not only that, but something else was strange about it. I looked and looked at her, trying to work it out. The dress hung differently. It was not the height and grandeur of Mrs Tobias alone, nor the fact that her bottom protruded more, it was the fact that she walked normally which finally struck me, through the parallel slats of the window. I had seen those dresses stagger and sway exaggeratedly, for even then my mother had to watch her feet to see where they were going, stooping slightly forward, swaying. So that the material of the skirt always hung forwards from the waistband, and the back became abnormally creased from so long being sat on. Mrs Tobias never sat: she squatted when she worked. They had no chairs, in any case.

She loved my dresses; she kept them all for best, for Sunday, my mother says.

We lost our rhythm somehow at the end. The heat became exasperating, the regularity of the rain a mockery of free will. Siesta turned into Malaria and I wondered whether I was sleeping or dying and why the room was shuddering all the time. There was always a strange tall man from the North at the French windows from the verandah with a basket of green bead necklaces made from broken beer bottles on his head, or a woman with dried fish for sale, who had walked from the coast.

Tommy dug holes and tunnels in the garden with his small friend he called Omo and came home one day to say that he had pointed his gun, made out of a stick, at two passing cars at the crossroads and they had really crashed. Everything became confused and suspended and there seemed to be daily more snakes by the back door, and more spiders who had somehow breached the mosquito netting to wobble over the pillow in the morning.

There was the longing for home and the almost resigned certainty, born out of heat-stroke and malarial tremors, that we would none of us survive to get there.

The small nightlamp throws light against the mosquito nets festooning our beds, Tommy's and mine. The night rituals have died away. My father simply kisses us and says Good-night, and goes. Tonight he won't. He is waiting. He has something sad to say, and he doesn't know how to say it.

Someone has died. He must fly home to England for the funeral. Your mother will stay, and there's Tobias to look after you.

A gloomy vacuum hung about the house for a week while he was gone and it felt as if the possibility of returning to where we really belonged was dying out, bit by bit.

She was on the verandah, smoking, vacant, fulsome, a blue silk shirtwaist dress stretched between mother-of-pearl buttons, calm and expectant, just after the rains when the air is cool and the spirits lift for a moment. The noise of the crickets, my father, lately returned, tuning in the radio inside. The world was rich and promising, and nothing was impossible. There was a distant thumping and singing from the huts at the end of the garden.

127

O-O-O-O solinam walinam
Kedim kede!
O-O-O-O solinam walinam
Kedim kede!

I can still see her from behind, looking into the garden of extraordinary tropical beauty, of pineapple, banana, geckoes and fruit-bats, the air washed by the six o'clock rains. What could be more celestial?

From here on her flesh would subside, falling away as surf from the sand, prematurely; the time-clock would turn into reverse. And she would insist that nothing was the matter, that there was nothing wrong with her.

It was just the Tropics.

11   *Trois Pistoles*

'I must go to the toilet and stretch my legs, Mum. Don't go away.'

She'll try not to.

'That's the spirit.'

Afterwards I go down the aisle towards the midships galley, past the sleeping passengers, to see the chaps. If I am no longer one of the Patients, I shall take advantage of it.

'Your mother seems to have cheered up,' says the Trained One, looking up from a magazine.

'We're rerunning old tapes; have got to the mid-sixties. Any bread and butter?'

'Puréed?'

'No, it's for me. I lost my dinner overboard, as it were.'

'You could have your breakfast. It's there. But then you wouldn't have any breakfast tomorrow.'

'How can you use the word "tomorrow" on an aeroplane? I'll have to live for the moment. Present breakfast rather than future food. Who knows, with the pilot incapable we may not survive until breakfast time.'

'We usually do.'

'That's not to say we shall,' I say, pulling out the tray with my seat number on it and taking off the tinfoil. 'Did you realize there is enough energy in your seat there to destroy the entire universe, should it spontaneously combust?'

'Is this a hijack?'

'Is this a croissant?' She laughs.

'It's high-class fare, y'know. Air Canada has gone bilingual with its breakfasts.'

'Where is the Steward?'

'Asleep someplace. Why, d'yer need him?'

'I never dreamt things were so casual on aeroplanes. I mean, so ordinary.'

'No. People think your feet never touch the ground, make-up permanently on.'

'Pilots permanently sober . . .'

'Exactly.'

'When is the dawn, then?'

'According to you, any time or never.'

'Ah yes, but *usually*?'

'About another hour and a half.' Her 'half' rhymes with 'transport caff'.

Another hour and a haff. Thirteen years to go, and another hour and a haff before the dawn might possibly break.

It is possible I may be able to keep it up.

'Where were we?'

Nigeria, she says, looking down at her feet, as if she had lost something. She says her legs have gone to sleep and could I rub her knees to restore circulation?

It's a long time since the singing of servants under tin roofs at the perimeter.

'Things were less artificial then; less additives in the food; not this pressurized rematerialization. We came home from Africa by boat, with the parrots, with our possessions, through time and over the sea.'

Stopping at increasingly less exotic places en route: Madeira, the Canaries. No such thing then as nuclear pollution, ecology, acid rain, or the endangered whales, or no such thing spoken of. Simply the sea and the countries in between: the colonies and the not. Sunsets as golden as a diplomatic passport.

* * *

A pantechnicon was just drawing up outside the Lewisham house when I left to walk down the road, through the bomb-site shortcut to the bus for the Grammar School. It was still strange to wear heavy woollen clothes, blazer and tie, and closed-in shoes after nearly two years of bare feet and sandals. Strange to sit on the top front of a double-decker bus with twenty or thirty others identically dressed. That dark afternoon was chess club or choir or netball practice and it was pitch black by the time I stood outside the dripping grey brick building and watched the headlights zigzagging across Catford High Street, waiting for my father to collect me to take me to the new house.

Tommy was on the back seat in his long grey shorts, with his knees newly bloodied. We sat in silence during the ride, wondering.

There were thirty-one steep steps up to the front door. The house itself was an imitation medieval castle, complete with tower (the dining room, my bedroom over) and leaded windows. At the back of the housecastle lay a garden which was only ever navigable by Tommy, his bucket-bred toads, and imaginary sure-footed goats who would not have looked out of place. A hundred types of fern and bracken grew on this hillside, for no human had ever managed to cultivate it.

What this house was, was a refusal to imagine the future. They should have bought a bungalow.

I didn't say anything.

– What do you think, Jane?

– What do *you* think, Mum?

– Well, it's a beautiful house, spectacular. I thought you would see that, being an artist.

What I could see, being an adolescent, and at the mercy of her every whim, was that she was happy, ecstatic. So I resolved to like the house, no matter how impossible it was from the practical point of view, or how pretentious from the aesthetic.

– It's a house I won't feel ashamed to entertain in.

131

– Yes, good.

Good. First things first.

– What do you think, Nan?

   – Your mother is ill, do be careful.

   – She has a quick temper, that I know.

   – Some things you will understand when you are older.

   – She shouts at me all the time.

   – Your mother is ill, be thoughtful.

   – I think she hates me.

   – That is only because you're adolescent.

   – So, it is I who am ill, is it?

   – No, you're alright. Only, your mother is ill, and you must make allowances.

I do make allowances. When I want to throw something out of anger or frustration, I make an allowance, a margin, and walk into it. It is not her fault she is ill. I go upstairs to the tower bedroom, sixty feet over the driveway, and lie on my bed and breathe deeply.

'JANE! Come down here at once. It's not fair to go off when you know I can't follow you.'

That's true. I must make further allowances. You can never walk out on an argument and wait for it to blow over, because she cannot follow you. So, back downstairs to stand again at the built-in oven in the kitchen where we were 'discussing' the state of my bedroom and how she was going to throw everything out of my window on to the tarmac of the driveway so far below unless I cleared it up immediately.

I let my thoughts drift by me. It is best – making allowances.

   – Do you want to live like a pig, is that it?

   – No, thank you. I do not want to live like a pig.

Too cool, too calm. She explodes – I saw it coming: by making allowances I have driven her, as all adolescents do, to the brink and over it.

   – I . AM . GOING . TO . DIE! Her right arm flashes briefly

into my field of vision and with unusual accuracy, though with the extraordinary *force* I know so well, she strikes me a stinging blow to the side of the head. I rocket into the oven door.

– THEN LET ME LIVE MY LIFE! I run upstairs again. On my bed I feel ashamed. I should have asked her *when*. Did she mean any minute now? Tomorrow? What did she mean? But for the millionth time, I had misunderstood.

Coming up the stairs is a thin, frightened little voice, sobbing. Can it be her?

– Janey, Janey!

No, I am absolutely not coming down again. You can ooch up on your bee-hind for all I care.

– Janey, I'm sorry. Forgive me. Of course I want you to live your life. I'm so proud of you. Oh, Janey, I don't know what I'm saying any more I am so ill.

Is it a ploy to get me down the stairs so she can cuff me again?

– Right, fine. Let's leave it there, can we?

– No, Janey, please.

Did she really apologize? Without any prompting from my father or her mother? Amazing! Am I winning the war, battle by battle?

Although we were swords-drawn inside the castle, there was no moat. Not really. People did come and visit us, voluntarily, and must have found us an odd group. My mother, weaving about now like someone permanently tipsy, my father, forever typing to a publisher's deadline in the small downstairs study behind the cloakroom, Nanny, often mistaken for the housekeeper, myself, Tommy and four animals. The parrots lived in an aviary suspended from the ceiling in the conservatory – the Falconry, as it were – just outside the kitchen, my brother finally got his dog – a corgi – and we had retrieved my cat from Gloria in Bedfordshire.

'Quite a zoo we had in Bromley, Mum.'

How I loved that house, she says.

* * *

133

– What's wrong with your mother?

– I don't know, but she's ill.

– Won't they tell you what it is?

– No. What difference would that make?

– Don't you care? Will she get better or die?

– I'm trying to grow up; I'm busy.

All these visitors must have left with the impression that eccentricity could be carried too far, even by expatriates returned home, for they had been exposed to such strange noises from all members of the family, *except* the parrots.

'It used to be so embarrassing, trying to get the parrots to perform when people came.'

No-one believed that they spoke, my mother says.

'But as soon as guests had escaped, out came torrents.'

The story of our lives from Nigeria to the present, complete and stereophonic, like the new record-players.

George would do the milkman puffing up the back stairs, Sam the chink of the milk bottles; George would do raised voices arguing in the kitchen, Sam the radio in the background and then, always dead on cue, crockery smashing, doors slamming. George would whistle for Fred, the dog; Sam would make the clicking sound of his claws on the quarry tiles. Often, they didn't need to provide the woof. Fred himself arrived, in reality, fooled into thinking my father had summoned him, and woofed. Sam woofed back. It is a wonder that dog retained his sanity.

– Nan! They are talking of buying you a bungalow, Uncle Jack and Dad. What does it mean?

– I might move to Bedford to be near Gloria and Arnold.

– Why, do they need you?

– For my retirement.

– Retirement? From what – us?

– Ha ha. You don't understand, lovie. You can come and stay with me. We'll have good times, and no-one to interfere with us. You, me and Tommy.

134

– Permanently?

– No, it'll be my house.

– I don't understand.

– Some things you'll . . .

– Oh, I know. When I'm older.

Where are the parrots now? asks my mother.

'In Yorkshire, with Uncle Dave.'

He's dead, she says, isn't he?

Yes, you're right. It must be another uncle.'

Along with the ghosts of Yorkshire pigeon-fancying days, in the pigeon-lofts where early in the morning, high above the cobbled streets of that small town, no doubt they can still be heard singing 'Way Down Upon De Swannee Ribber' in my twelve-year-old voice which I no longer have, or multiplication tables in Tommy's voice before it broke, to the astonishment of passing workmen on their way to mill or pit.

But most poignant of all is the thought of them saying in her old, clear voice, such catch phrases as 'better late than never', 'charity begins at home' and 'birds of a feather'.

'They'll still be saying your proverbs, Mum, a hundred years from now when we're all pushing up the daisies.'

God forbid, she says.

God forbid what?

That we keep the past alive? Where is the past? It has not gone anywhere, for it cannot move; it has no such power. Somewhere in another dimension, those parrots are still suspended over the conservatory calling and whistling for the dog, who, being unable to distinguish the parrot from the human voice (because they are indistinguishable) will come running, barking, from his basket in the kitchen, puzzled. Again and again.

And Uncle Dave has always just died. My father has always just missed the funeral. We travel endlessly over the moors in our Ford Zephyr, almost obliterating the stone front of Aunty Edith's cottage by parking alongside it, in the narrow street.

– Eh if tha'd bin 'ere, she says. Tears stand in her pale blue eyes. She strokes her apron down, pauses, throws her wobbly arms around my father. They cry together, rock. Like a mother and her son. The sky is low and grey over the cobbled yard. We stand with my mother, a few yards off. Excluded. My father dissolves into Aunty Edith. Here he belongs.

In his past. Here where the small motherless boy was absorbed back into the larger family, the tribe, and read Rider Haggard and John Buchan curled up by the grate where the everlasting kettle hissed its welcome to the aunts from next door and the uncles from down the road. Under the clouds of pipe smoke cut with cabbage leaf from the allotments, under the gaslights, by the basins of boiled water with soot floating on the rim, the inedible crusts of pork-pies flung surreptitiously into the fire.

Here he had grown, an exotic weed between the solid rocks of Uncle Dave and Aunty Edith and Aunty Lett.

I too pulled at the voluminous skirts of this same matriarch, in the ancient days, before memory has crystallized,with my band of Indians she 'minded' for me by the fire in her back room, keeping them warm.

– Tha sleeps wi' arms in air, she told me.

– I do not, aunty.

– Tha does. I seen thee.

– Why, then?

– Eh, stop thy natterin' and go t'wish t'uncle John goonayt.

– I can't. He doesn't speak English. He can't understand me, nor I him.

– 'E speaks no different from thy Dad did when 'e were one of us.

I can still remember her wheezy, floury laughter, her coal-smudged hands.

– Ee our John, this lass says as tha doan speak English!

– Auweelthacannathenoonerthat!

136

Never a word passed, comprehended, between us.

His wife, Aunty Lett, cannot die: she is not mortal. She is Life itself. Surely all Life emanates from somewhere under her tent-sized apron?

When she did 'pass o'er', for no-one had the courage, or the pessimism, to call it death, my father flew back from Nigeria for the funeral, by himself. But he did not make it to Uncle Dave's passing over. Uncle Dave was not life itself.

– He'd a bad time, tha knows. He asked for thee.

He flinches. She will spare him nothing. She knows that he knows that it is not love to spare him, that there is no sparing – only detail upon detail etched out in gruesome euphemism. She shares out her overflowing grief with the only person Dave fathered, with his only 'child'.

– It mun be our Jane! She do favour our Sarah.

Another one who died young: my father's mother. She has been gone long enough, been galloped far enough off by the consumption, to have joined those ranks of the dead who have 'come back' and share a pipe with the living, though invisible. They are all mixed up with the living, and with the imaginary – my band of Indians, for instance. Warming all their buttocks against the range in the back room. Come back in out of the cold, all our loved ones.

– Oh, ay, she favours our Sarah, no mistake.

My mother purses her lips, and moves her jaw from side to side.

– She has my mother's auburn hair, actually.

My father's relatives do not use words like 'actually'. They survey my mother, over the crisps, pork pies, Battenburg cake, bought and 'processed' food of which my mother disapproves.

She is too delicate, too fine, too fiery and too Southern; there is no strength, no stability, no wholesomeness in her. But they are sorry to hear she is ill, though sorrow is only a way of life, and does not call for any outbursts of protest. What is, is.

– Are you nursing still, Charlotte?

– No, I've had to abandon it.

– Ay, that's right; for the best.

137

Growing, courting, wedding, expecting, nursing, rearing,working and dying – here time passes under the indifferent gaze of an incomprehensible God, second cousin to the Nigerian one, until the last pipe fizzles out under the Road Finish sign by some pond or other.

– Think of your poor mother, with you two to look after.
   – Why? Is it my fault?
   – Just be as helpful as you can, and don't answer back. You're both coming to stay with me for three weeks.
   – Really! Why?
   – Haven't they told you?
Three weeks of shelter from the storm: life in a vacuum.

When my parents returned from Canada they had arranged to have a house custom-built, with no steps, and my father had accepted a post at a Canadian university.

We didn't really travel to Canada in a submarine but my memories give that feeling. As if we dived into greyness infinite and held our breaths for eleven days and resurfaced in Halifax, Nova Scotia. It is always a grim passage, crossing the Atlantic; no wonder we do it by aeroplane now. You can't even contemplate enjoying it – the weather and the waves are unremittingly fierce and grey. This feeling of alienation was further reinforced by the fact that on the *Maasdam* all the announcements were in Dutch. I can still say 'Beef tea will not be served on the deck this morning, owing to the severity of the weather' in Dutch.
   There is simply one giant omission on this trip – coasts. Only bridgeable spans are meant to be crossed.

That bridge spans the Bay, my father was saying, pointing out of the picture-window of a motel bedroom on the

Bay between Halifax and Dartmouth, our temporary home while our new house was being built. My mother was lying down 'fuming'. Why had he directed the taxi through Halifax's only ten slums? Why had he not brought us the scenic route?

– They don't want to know *that*! Take them to the swimming pool, she shouted from the other room. He continued, about the twin cities, about an explosion during the war in the Bay which had lifted people half a mile, some of whom had survived.

About how the bodies from the Titanic had been washed up along the beach of that same Bay and buried down there in anonymous graves. It was just what we wanted to know: how did this place fit in to the rest of the world? Where were we?

Launching out from the Bay-side motel, we visited the site of our new house. The foundations were already there. The trees had been felled to make a clearing, and three workmen, Otis and his two assistants, were seated on a log, comparing their lunch-pails.

– Whatcha got there, Otis?

– Ham. Whatcha got?

– Peanut budder and jelly.

Otis and my father were already friends. They discussed handrails and floor surfaces and tile colours and bathroom fittings, there in the middle of the woods and the dirt. My mother, now unable to stand without one of us supporting her, queried everything, questioned everything, and always prevailed.

While this house was being built in Halifax, we were homeless, so we went to Ottawa to see her older sister, Babs. I had seen her before but I didn't remember her. Because she had only ever been alluded to, never spoken of directly, and because Nanny was unwilling to give details of why she had twice flown to Canada as an emergency to take care of Babs, though my mother finally told me that Babs had miscarried two pregnancies, Babs had naturally become something of a Mysterious Person to me.

139

The idea was that we would accompany her on her annual escape from the Ontarian heat to her cottage at Trois Pistoles, a small settlement on the St Lawrence for a thousand other escapees, complete with its own Summer School.

'First time I met Babs, that summer, at the cottage.'

No, no, says my mother, she came over to England when you were small, many times.

'But I can't remember that.'

It was the impression she made then that was so overwhelming. My mother would *like* to forget.

Perhaps I should let her?

Where Gloria was scratchy, nervous, unsure, depressed, this other older sister was ebullient, confident, always laughing. Beautiful too: a film-star face from the forties movies with short dark curly hair, large made-up eyes, and an endearingly original hairline, which came down to an arrow-point on one side of her forehead. Her voice was deep and hardly distorted at all. She would enunciate words with the exaggerated stage-talk of the elocution teacher. And she walked on her own. Her husband, Uncle Jack, let her struggle and weave about on fashionable high heels with a man's stout walking stick. The struggle is good for her, he seemed to say, and she was thriving on it: at forty-two she still looked thirty.

It was hard, at fourteen, not to reach the conclusion that Babs was better than my mother because my mother had us. Babs was childless, and better for it, though her affliction was identical.

Babs was better than my mother at everything except reproduction. She cooked well, entertained brilliantly, spoke better in English *and* French, walked independently, drove a car still, though Heaven help any elderly pedestrians relying on the speed and accuracy of her reactions. My mother had given up driving some time ago.

She whizzed around, breaking things, laughing, glittering, bejewelled: a person out of the ordinary but refusing to be put down.

'Aunty Babs presented me with a doll about three feet high, which she had bought with Green Shield stamps. Janey is a bit old for dolls – how you laughed!' – from the depths of a Liberty-print armchair where she had been put, and was obliged to stay until my father or I should give her an arm.

– I get so tired, don't you darling? said Babs, on her knees in front of the low-level drinks cabinet, pouring everyone drinks with two hands gripped tightly on each bottle, concentrating as hard as the women who make circuits in the Far East. And only about a quarter of a pint of various liquids ended up on the tray beneath: to me, a miracle.

– You seem so well, Aunty, I said.

– No, darling, not well, she replied, very, very ill.

What I'd meant to say was happy, but that word is like a waiter: never there when needed.

Her vocabulary was astonishing: if she described someone as 'hairy' and you thought she'd said 'very' she would come out with a veritable thesaurus of alternatives: hirsute, simian, until you got it, or looked it up.

Coping with illness by virtue of happiness.

She showed me the twin beds she and her husband slept in. I was amazed. Had they no children then because they didn't 'love' each other? I wondered. She explained that her noises at night kept Jack awake, so they slept separately for both their sakes.

– Aren't they gorgeous lace covers, Jane? Shall I leave them to you in my Will?

I heard my mother's noises for the first time when we got to Trois Pistoles, to the cottage, the following day, since their bedroom was separated from mine only by a thin curtain. I must have heard it before; I must have done.

'The "cottage" was really a wooden shack with all the latest amenities: freezer, television.'

141

There didn't seem to be any locals on this stretch of the shingly riverside, only rows and rows of rich Ontarians, summering. To escape the heat and humidity inland, they had come for miles with their children, pets, tents, boats, and barbecue equipment. Babs followed us the next day with a car full of frozen provisions, reading matter, records, all the essentials of civilized life.

And she made that long journey *on her own*, for her husband was still working.

The river lapped at the shingle continuously, punctuating the talk inside the shack, the thin walls could not keep out the insistent close sound of the tidal river.

Something along the banks of the St Lawrence, something in bloom, whether grass or flower, or bush, had it in for me. No sooner had I arrived than my eyelids became swollen, and I began to sneeze violently. My lips and throat itched and breathing was only slightly less difficult than eating. My mother looked up 'antihistamine' in the English-French dictionary and sent my father to buy some from Le Drugstore in Trois Pistoles. About twenty minutes after swallowing the first capsule, the relief of being able to see and breathe again was so overwhelming that I took two deep breaths and fell asleep, where I was, on an armchair.

This became the pattern for the next few days. I would awake, wheeze, gasp, swallow a pill, yawn and go back to sleep. This was too much for my mother. She informed my father and Aunty Babs that I was *not* to be allowed to sleep all day. They pointed out, my father gently, and Babs less so, that antihistamine had a sedative effect and I had no option but to lose consciousness.

Unfortunately it was Matters Medical and no amount of arguing on their side made any difference. She pointed out to them that people at work did not take the summer off because of hay fever, and they replied that since I was not at work and did not *need* to earn my living, this fact was not relevant. All this I vaguely heard in the stupor between doses, through the curtain dividing the sleeping areas from the sitting area.

Finally Babs prevailed by saying that she would see to it that I had something which was worth conquering drowsiness *for*.

I thought this was extremely generous of Babs since she had been accused not only of Total Ignorance on Matters Medical (weren't we all?) but also of not knowing anything about children, being childless, which seemed unnecessarily cruel.

Babs had seen some of my sketches of the Dartmouth Bridge and surrounding woodlands and thought I could foster my talent at the local Art School, part of the University of Western Ontario. It was intended for university students, but Babs was undaunted by small details like this, and phoned the Principal for an appointment the next morning.

My most vivid memory of this terrible incident is just *before* it happened. This is common with traumas: the event itself is hazy while the preceding moments stand out clearly. The mind defends itself, it seems, against pain by diffusing it into 'bits'.

The first 'bit' is simply that Aunty Babs and I crossed a road, having parked the car. Babs' idea of parking the car was gently to hurl the machine, a large American car, from the bumper in front to the bumper behind, until she was more or less level with the pavement, which she called the 'sidewalk'.

I wasn't to help her out of the car. I had to stand back and watch her straining and gripping and pulling herself out with the thick stick under her armpit. I was allowed to lock the car for her.

We waited on the sidewalk, until Babs could wait no longer: about seventy seconds.

– You will have grown up by the time we get across this road, she said. We started across, the traffic no thinner than before. I was terrified: what if she should

143

fall? She couldn't run; I would have to run away and leave her to be run over.

And I wasn't even to support her under the arm. We walked.

– The roads are wide here, don't worry, she said, pedestrians have the right of way at corners in this country. She was talking too of how tall my little brother was. Strange, she was saying, because neither of my parents were very tall. My Uncle Owen in Yorkshire is nearly seven feet, I said, giantism is it called?

The cars stopped, screeching, slithering, colliding. She smiled at them her Hollywood smile, saying to me at the same time, between clenched teeth, can't they see the stick, the morons?

Into a large building with stairs. This is the next 'bit': I wasn't to help her up. She ooched up them, breathing hard, smiling, but talking out of the question.

– Stop frowning; it spoils your looks, she said when she reached the top.

The Principal was expecting us. He gave a faint bow and said, and here comes the haze, something like:

– Car accident, was it? pointing to the stick.

– No, no, she beamed, taking breath, a hereditary condition.

What happened then? A fog descended. She was introducing her niece to him, and they were speaking of my talent and my desire to paint and the art course and Monsieur Papke, who would nurture . . . and on and on.

Hereditary.

Inherited.

Me.

They might have handed me a live hand-grenade with the pin out and I would have been in a lesser state of shock.

The colour of my life was never the same from this moment onwards: the future had become a threat, not a promise.

*   *   *

I hardly spoke that summer. I painted, under the super-
vision of Monsieur Papke who was astonished at the
tragedy as he called it in my water and trees and *'choses
simples,'* the investment of horror in the simple land-
scapes of *la belle Province*.

Trois Pistoles: three loaded guns: the Past, the Present,
and the Future. Only the Future was always loaded and
now it was cocked, and turned towards me.

12   Settling up

There is a Law of the Universe which presents a would-be passenger who has been waiting forty minutes for a bus with three; it creates a need for the ten rubber bands you just (ruthlessly) threw out, the newspapers you just burnt. This Law even holds many thousands of feet up in the air, for it has just come into effect on the aeroplane – two people, and then two more, struggle, clench-kneed, past us towards the toilets and form a queue behind us.

They were waiting for the lights, my mother says.

Sad, how clever she still is; I hadn't thought of that.

But then I don't; I never expect one thing to follow on from another. I never expected that by the time we returned to Halifax from Quebec our house would be complete.

'Strange seeing all that old-fashioned English furniture and African bric-à-brac in our brand new ranch-style house in Halifax.'

You said it made you feel at home, she says.

I probably said that, for some reason.

Even more astonishing was the fact that the surrounding woods from which a small gap had initially been made for our house had almost disappeared, to make way for a whole curving road of similar houses, all very slightly different, each with its own driveway, carport, and its own colour of wooden weather-board facing. Telephone wires bisected the sky, and a fire hydrant or two had appeared by the side of what would very shortly

146

be a road. I couldn't help being reminded of a campus in the Nigerian bush, now burnt to the ground in the Biafran War.

– Which bit is my garden, and which bit is yours? my father asked our neighbour.

– I guess this bit behind my house is mine, and the bit behind yerr house is yerrs, if ya wanna think of it that way, he replied.

– Can't we tell exactly, then?

– Why d'yer need ta know?

– I have to protect my dog and have some privacy.

– Yerr dog and yerr children are welcome to play on my bit, I don't mind.

But his children and his dog walked on the sweet pea seedlings once too often, and had worn a rutted path across our property on their short-cut way home from school before my father was driven, by guess whom, to erect a nine-foot-high larch-lap fence around what he assumed to be the extent of our property. The neighbours all dismissed us as eccentric English people who grew roses, and socially we were finished.

The scent of barbecues and the sound of teenage voices calling each other across the open expanses of eight backyards uncharted by fence or boundary sometimes wafted down through the vent in my basement bedroom window.

From where I heard her calling and calling over and over again, when she was in this house without my father, for Tom and me, and our pretending not to hear her, not wanting to go and 'keep her company'. One day, when there was only me downstairs she must have got down on her bottom with the broom, and passed slowly, destructively, through the ironically-named 'rumpus room', still calling, smashing and ripping my pictures as she went past them – my pictures for the school Project which were ranged, drying on easels. And on down the corridor to my room, where she hammered and hammered on my locked door with the broom. Just wait till he gets home and hears about this!

147

No.

Wrong.

Who cares about your bloody Art, when your mother was alone and distressed?

They who smiled proudly at the Open Day when my series of paintings illustrating 'Upon Westminster Bridge' were prominently displayed. The professor with his sweet ailing wife draped on his arm gazes up approvingly at the work of his talented daughter (such a comfort to them, no doubt), who behaved rather badly at the Open Day, and would not answer any questions put to her.

Outside the world is peaceful, Canadian, materialistic, modern, civilized. Inside this goddamn custom-designed bungalow, it is medieval, cruel and warlike. There is a state of siege between the basement and the first-floor levels. I try to escape in the morning without passing through the kitchen and am accused of jeopardising my health by not eating breakfast deliberately so that my mother would have a wretched time nursing me, when she was the one needing attention. There was no way of winning and every way to lose.

She went with my father to a psychiatrist who told her she was not mad. Coming home she told me with great relief that she was not mad. Isn't that wonderful?

Great, now you can order an appropriate Spring Wardrobe from the Simpson Sears Catalogue. You won't have to limit yourself to strait-jackets, handcuffs and so on, you can really go *mad*!

What are you supposed to say? Not mad – ah, good. So pleased. Then that wild, possessed look in your eyes is intended for the excessive motes of dust on the flock wallpaper behind me, rather than me, is it? I see, just checking.

Still, if not mad, then bad? If not mad, then unforgivable. Oh, I nearly forgot, for one millipercentile of a millisecond of my waking existence, that you're ill. Of course, silly me. We must make allowances.

The reason she is not in need of psychiatric help is that she simply has a problem that she needs to solve. Your illness, is it?

– No, it's you.

I knew it. I always knew it was my fault.

– My problem is that I'm worried that you'll hate me. You don't hate me, do you?

– No, of course not, I say to the entire family assembled to hear the Good News of her Sanity. No, of course not. No.

And run down into the basement after she has said,

– Oh, that's alright then, that's settled then. Down to cry into my pillow and shout I HATE YOU I HATE YOU I HATE YOU until my throat is burning and dry and choked.

You see, Mr Psychiatrist, unfortunately my problem is that I'm worried that what worries my mother is the Absolute Truth, and you can't settle that away.

And make a mental note for the future to send a set of jump leads to that psychiatrist next Christmas, so he can restart his brain from someone else's.

The incredible truth is that there were still Good Times at all. And yet there were.

'Remember going back to England that first summer and already finding it so changed?'

Everything was changing, the world over, and rapidly. We sat in the darkened front room of Nanny's bungalow in Northampton, the sun blazing outside, with the curtains drawn, watching the first man land on the moon, live. My father insisted on us watching it. It was History, he said, perhaps the biggest event which would happen in our lifetimes. Impressed, we stopped rummaging in the kitchen for another yoghurt – a new invention too, flavoured yoghurt in cartons – and sat. At first I thought it was badly shot, some sort of X-ray film, fiction. But gradually it dawned on us all what we were seeing and there was no getting up again until it was all over.

'They finally landed a man on the moon.'

We watched it on television at Nanny's, she says.

And then my mother said,

– They should have spent all that money on the starving children all over the world instead of wasting it on a stupid expedition. I thought, what a crass thing to say when we had just witnessed a massive breakthrough in man's exploration of the frontiers of the universe. But, to my surprise, my father nodded.

– You've got a point there, of course.

'That was a good summer, Mum. We went round stately homes, and the Aquadrome, and horse riding.' All those English things you do when you are staying at someone else's house.

Nanny was getting older, was not enjoying living on her own, and had noticed mysterious cracks in all her ceilings.

There were open-ended conversations as we left, between the three of them:

– Well, if it doesn't work . . .

– Yes, you never know . . .

– . . . draw your pension anywhere.

Then, back in Halifax, Good Times became scarcer and scarcer. We went to our new schools, Tom and I, and both adopted Canadian accents which we guiltily abandoned as we walked through the front door. And the snow fell in November and stayed until June.

'Skating on Chocolate Lake – what winters in Canada!'

My skates were white figure-skates, Tom's black hockey boots, my father's a compromise grown-up boot. We always parked on the deserted road by the side of the lake.

– Just do my test, he'd say, and we had to hunt for the biggest rock we could lift. He hurled it at the ice. Either it crashed in or bounced and skidded off towards the far shore.

One day it was ambiguous. It landed safely but a long

crack appeared by the side of where it had first hit the ice. We stood. She wound down her window.

– Can't you make a simple decision?

We stood, waiting for a decision, getting cold in the air drifting off the ice, as we were not moving. Only moving keeps you warm once you are out of the car. There were stories about people leaving their broken-down cars and dying from exposure in twenty minutes. There was a grinding noise from the sky, a great rumbling, and not a cloud in sight. Then we saw it – a large ski-plane, coming straight for us. It landed on the frozen lake, quite near us, and several tons of metal shuddered into silence on the ice we feared to tread on. How we laughed. The ice was about four inches thick; the boulders must have been getting bigger and heavier, the test harder, as Tom grew beefier and found bigger rocks.

You could get out of range of the Midas eyes for a while in the frosty air. Just a white clouded window in a barely perceptible car, a small dark square against the immense white. And skate until the sweat poured down between the woollen edges of every garment, so that you could have stripped down to a leotard by the end, been free and almost naked and frozen to death in the middle of nowhere as the puck sped between the men of the family further on, between the trees caught in autumnal floods and frozen all winter. How I cherished that solitude on the ice. The claustrophobic's dream: an eternity of ice as far as the horizon and only trees beyond, with the odd plane, a promise of a larger world, landing nearby.

Then back into the snug of the car where her impatience had steamed the windows for over an hour, to speed back down the Bicentennial Highway, past the Airport, always in the process of being built or rebuilt.

Once Nanny had sold her house, subsidence and all, and come out to join us, my mother didn't have to come with us; she stayed at home. Nanny did not always manage to live peacefully with us. Then she would go across the Bay to Dartmouth and stay with Gloria and Arnold who had also emigrated. When she had fallen out with them, or they with her, she would return to us. She took part in all battles, though she was getting too old for it. I don't know what battles she had with Gloria but it was always a great relief when she left them, and a great relief when she returned to them. Some mornings I would wake and not know for sure whether Nanny was living with us or not.

There is no *winning* a battle, when the adversary is so weak, so enfeebled, so to be pitied.

Soon it was the War of the Wheelchair. It meant admitting that her disability was permanent. No more 'You'll get better, Mum, look at you: much perkier than yesterday'. It meant saying, this is how you are, and it will get worse, so let's put you on wheels. You have got to let us push you around literally, though God knows no-one ever got the chance to do it metaphorically, not without major fallout.

We should just 'park' her somewhere, she said. It was like surrendering her independence, her freedom, to be in a wheelchair. The freedom to fall and cry and break things. Like saying that to feed the starving is to deny them the freedom to die. But finally the cruellest objection of them all, 'I'm not a baby and I don't want a pram!' What can you say to that one?

We all looked at each other, lost between Truth and Compassion.

The man who came from the Everest Wheelchair and Disabled Aids firm said that she would be in good company and named famous people now confined to wheelchairs; Everest wheelchairs of course. It was his job, but he did it well. We had all the brochures, and a wheelchair with a motor to let her have a 'go' in. She zoomed around alarmingly, pleased, like a child with a toy, or . . .

He also pointed out that she was not totally disabled

and would be able to choose when to use it and when not. If she was not totally disabled, I wanted to know, but did not ask, what was his definition of 'totally'? He flattered her, cajoled, spoke terms with my father, and the chair was ordered.

She phoned her sister, Gloria, and told her. Gloria was delighted and came round to talk about it at length. It was an opportunity for a great many home-truths to be said on both sides: they agreed that now was the time to cut one's coat according to the cloth, that discretion was the better part of valour, and necessity the mother of newfangled inventions, and concluded that it was a long lane which had no turning, and a wheelchair with power-steering was proof of this.

Riding on this triumph of commonsense over neurosis, attempts were made thereafter to hire people as well as machines: money was never the prah'blem. I was away at university when the first one came. She was middle-aged, hard as nails and excellent. She was the sort of housekeeper my mother would have been without her disease. They got on like opposing Superpowers: not at all. My father spoke highly of her on the phone to me, and then fired her.

The prah'blem here was that Mrs Whatever gave my father and Tom (and even myself) the opportunity to be somewhere else without a guilty conscience; to be 'downstairs' as it were, ignoring her righteously. It meant my father did not always have to come home for lunch, nor always leave the office at the stroke of five; he could afford to exchange a few words with a colleague. Tom could afford to play his three-day-long War Games with his friends at their houses, could join the school band and play the trumpet, could go away for chess championships overnight.

But Mrs Whatever had an infinite capacity for enduring insult (no doubt she too had 'seen worse'), which was her downfall. My mother was used to wounding easily with a few well-chosen words. These words may have

153

been distorted but they were exquisitely well chosen! The woman was too well armed. They should have had a young Filipino girl my mother could have terrified, someone who could not operate a vacuum cleaner without instruction. Her incompetence would then have allowed my mother the total domination she so desired, in all her relationships.

But my mother was too disabled to be left in the sole charge of an incompetent. At any moment she might need to be rescued, resuscitated, have clothes covered in scalding coffee whipped off her.

'You had a succession of housekeepers, I believe. I don't think I ever met any of them.'

You didn't miss much, she says. They were *awful*.

'Well you can't get good staff any more, Mum. Well-known fact.'

They treated me like an idiot, she says, and lied to your father about me; they were so deceitful.

Oh, I can imagine it: the crimes and counter-crimes and accusations. Fire her, fire her, or I'll . . .

Outside was the normal world in the form of Canada: the world where people get the blues, feel off-colour, upset, bored, restless; where they speculate and have peripheral thoughts; where Survival is no issue; where people think about clothes, movies, fashion, go steady, have regular rows, and recover from them; where people have 'a bit of a giggle' or phone each other up for a chat.

Inside was the bitter struggle for survival, interspersed with moments of intense awareness vouchsafed to the adolescent alone, of the futility of the universe, so that I sometimes felt a solidarity with the High-Rise dwellers uptown who threw dogs and relatives out of their windows and all those who, with battered emotions, seek a final solution.

If I survive to be old, I shall never tax the young with excessive self-pity, for there is no consolation in youth itself.

* * *

'Do you remember Mrs E, who used to come and take you out? Never stopped speaking, even to breathe?'

She spoke nonsense, though, says my mother, turning away towards the aisle, as if all the Norms here would only speak nonsense if woken and applied to for some conversation.

Perhaps I should stop now. Perhaps this is as far as we can go?

It was inevitable that she should be spotted as someone's ideal captive audience. What sort of people would befriend her now; she was at the mercy of whoever would. Apart from the clergy, that is, and she even suspected their motives. Are they after some charity, she'd say, we've given already through Oxfam. We don't want to subsidize crazies who go out to convert the darkies. Groucho Marx might have hailed her as the sole member of the only club which would have her as a member.

'Art Exhibitions, wasn't it, where she criticised the pictures openly and loudly?'

There is no response. Perhaps she spoke openly and loudly of other, more interesting things, when they were alone together. Who knows?

'About that time Tom built himself his own "quarters" in the basement so that you wouldn't have to put up with his stereo or his trumpet practice.'

He and my father, in the basement of the house, not the house Otis had built between sandwiches, but the one nearer to town, in the thick of it. A house with a history, and a tunnel to somewhere which had been bricked up and made into a downstairs bathroom.

'Brilliant place: a whole apartment out of a garage and the boiler room.'

Meanwhile the whole world she might have phoned from the lone splendour of her upstairs armchair went Permanent Engaged and Rang Off.

Fight or flight. I had flown to university. Tom had to stay and fight because he was too young to go, and staying, desired oblivion, for he was expected to behave

155

as if he was adult enough to leave, without being allowed to do so. His best friend at this time was the son of a couple one of whom was alcoholic and one of whom was dying of cancer. Surely the only other person in the world who could have felt at home *chez nous*, or rather *chez the* basement apartment.

My heart aches at the treatment he received from her, and though I can forgive now a lot of what she did to me, for she was ill, under gigantic stress and unfit for it, I can't yet forgive her what she did to him.

It was not one overriding, terrible thing: it was a slow and awful campaign to undermine his entire life so that he would cease to function as fully as she.

'Tom used to be able to climb over the back fence at that house and into the school grounds, only leaving the house when he heard the bell for assembly.'

Tom is sitting on the floor with a War Game spread before him: he is both the Allies and the Third Reich. He is at war with himself in a game of sufficiently complex strategy to give him the intellectual oblivion he needs. I am sitting reading on the sofa, far away on the other side of the long room. She is smoking by the lamp, in her armchair, the wheelchair folded against the wall behind her. She will not read her book. She is looking from one of us to the other, making us feel uncomfortable. The veins in her neck are blue, taut and bulging as she nurses her rage.

– Tell him to stop that!

– Stop what? He's only playing.

– The mess! He's got to clear it up now.

– Why? He hasn't finished.

– I. SAID. TELL. HIM. TO. STOP. IT. NOW.

– You tell him. I don't want him to stop.

– Thomas, I'm warning you. Just wait till your father gets home. He doesn't move. He is concentrating on the probability of the dice he has just thrown, working it out.

– Leave me alone, he says. Not 'piss off' or 'fuck off' or any of the things he will later tell his friends at school with bravado, that he said.

156

– YOU'VE DONE IT NOW she shouts, and throws her cigarette at him. Of course, it misses, but we both jump to retrieve it, as we often have to for more innocent losses, and in the confusion, she hurls herself out of the chair onto the board, upsetting the pieces, ruining the War.

– *Now* will you clear it up and sweep the floor? Tom leaves, for he knows, even at ten, that this is the best punishment he can inflict on her, to disappear into the margin. He goes back downstairs to his den and I clear it up, but I won't sweep the floor, won't get her a 'nice cup of tea' until my father returns to a barrage of imaginary crimes his son has committed. I only raise my eyebrows to his questioning look and he knows what has happened as if he had seen it on film. And part of the crime here is mine, mine and my father's: we assume that the ten-year-old Tom knows what has happened, that he too can be philosophical about it. We treat him with all the respect due to a suffering adult rather than the understanding due to a child.

I could make the tea and make the beds, but I could not make it right for Tom. Only a mother could have done that, and I was not qualified, not willing.

So I made the dinner and she could not eat it, for the food was deliberately difficult to eat, and I defended myself a little as a gesture, to give her the impression that it still mattered what she thought, though it hardly does any more. I call this Survival Credibility. My university friends call it English Reserve. So the meal was survived, and the washing up done and I felt that somewhere there were people who were happy, there must be.

She must go to a nursing home, we tell our father. Our father who art increasingly in the world of his work, and who can blame him? In a way, we don't. Work is, after all, a more acceptable escape, a better 'fix' than alcohol or heroin.

Only, even saying it seems like disloyalty, like unconscionable daring. The thought of her in a nursing home is like the thought of men living permanently on Mars; too odd to contemplate. And the thought of suggesting it to her is like the thought of confessing your sins on satellite television, naked.

And yet it is the *only* solution. Only, but Machiavellian. We must depose the Sick Queen, for her own good, and ours, and it involves bloodshed, metaphorically. None of us are quite brave enough to do it. Not in cold blood. In the heat of the moment, you could, any of you, kick under the drowning victim who is pulling you under. There is no point in your both dying; it is instinctive.

We cannot discuss this with my father, for there are strict rules of assembly in this monarchy: no two or more people may congregate out of my mother's earshot, ever. I wonder if there are any other families in the wide world who have had to resort to speaking to each other on public telephones in times of crisis, when living in the same house?

At such times, or other, stolen 'on pretext' times, when my father can speak, he talks of 'where his loyalties lie' and is torn to shreds, trying to do the right, best thing for everyone; himself least of all. Everyone is so sympathetic, so kind, and so unaware of the tenth part of the horror he lives with.

He is eight minutes late home. Traffic! Ha. She knows, and he need not think she doesn't, of the vile, corrupt, evil practices in which he is engaged. She knows everything. Can he deny it? Sometimes, to vary the pattern, or perhaps to lift her spirits, I have heard him confess to making love to four secretaries, murdering three hippies mooching around the university, having stolen liquor from two Liquor Commissions and driven through a red light. Yes, I did all that.

There is a gap. Tom and I giggle, waiting for her to laugh. She doesn't.

Softly, almost inaudibly, she says, very clever, *very* clever.

A small thing goes right, a small smile surfaces. Perhaps – ecstasy as readily available as despair – everything will be alright, will mend, though not mother.

Perhaps ... and then down again, for underlying everything, the country of the Sick Queen is in famine, is over.

Over. Everything Finish.

The only non-controversial topic is the dog, Fred.

We talk endlessly about Fred, finding more things to say about a mere dog than you'd think was possible.

Only, some other element is needed, to elicit the instinctive response, to make it alright to deal the knock-out kick with a good conscience.

Grand sentiment and loyalty are getting us nowhere, say Tom and I, trying to move from the old dispensation, the Sick Province, to the new, Canada. Glimpses of the new world are tantalizingly close, just out of reach.

'You had wonderful departmental parties. Quite the hostess, you were.'

Someone had to do it, she says, smiling smugly, meaning that only she *could*.

She cannot wear the little black dress any more – it hangs from her like a jumble-sale dress. She has been zipped into a blue polyester dress with a jacket over it which makes her look an almost normal shape. Carried downstairs by my father to the kitchen where I have applied the lipstick, wrongly, wiped it off, presented her with the mirror and done it again.

I have set up the lemon mousse-making equipment as if for a three-year-old. The lemons are cut and a pyramid shape has been gouged out (discreetly) so that she will have little trouble pushing them down onto the lemon squeezer. The sugar is measured, the butter weighed and ready, within the small arc of an arm's reach from the wheelchair. Kitchens with units the normal height are impossible for people in wheelchairs – they can only use the first ten inches of the surface. Tommy has brought the wooden box to raise the level of the chair from below. We raise her.

Acres of kitchen paper available to mop up two thirds of the juice which will rocket on to the surface when she presses the fruit too hard. I have the juice of four lemons squeezed, in the fridge ready.

It is far more trouble than it's worth, I could have made the mousse in ten minutes. She knows this. We all know this. But she must *make* some of the food. The guests will be told this. Charlie made the mousse herself. She didn't, did she?

You are wonderful, Charlie, so *brave*. After ten minutes of 'bravery' she gives up and my father helps her sip sherry. I clear the mess, make the mousse and retire to drink something pilfered from the boxes inside the back door. The strange thing is, all this trouble I go to, all that tenderness with which I guide her hand to the spoon and sugar bowl, seems to make her hate me even more fiercely. Why?

There is no Nanny to roll and boil and bake, and so, apart from the historic mousse, the rest of the food is the frozen, prepackaged, processed food my mother so despised in her youth, on which we are forced to live, not merely entertain. Food is only fuel, she says now. That's all. Take it or leave it.

She usually leaves it; especially if I have prepared it.

But it's nobody's fault. No one is to blame.

Tom, who is grown up now, doesn't find it possible to blame no-one. So he blames you. You sitting there in your turquoise get-up. People have been ill before without being cruel. In the history of the world mothers were ill, died, and still loved their sons. He might come to see you, if you live to settle in the nursing home, but I doubt it. If he does, expect no sympathy, no compromise. You don't deserve it. You told him to go play in the traffic, your own son, and he does not weep for it, as I do still, but has hardened himself against you, as he has had to, to survive, to grow up.

'Having it out clears the air, you used to say.'

No response.

Poisonous things she said cannot be unsaid. The heat of the moment melted the delicate filigree of relationships into a molten blob. The names she called me when I was only twelve, thirteen, fourteen; dreadful, incomprehensible dirty names. Why should she do that? Whatever did we do to deserve that treatment, except walk about on our own two feet when she could not?

'Oh Mummy . . .' I am lost.

What is it? she asks, genuinely surprised at the tears appearing suddenly on my side of the armrest; all *normal* people have rows, it's only natural, she says.

'The question is really, whether you loved us, not . . .'

Don't be stupid, she warns, her face screwed into agony, she *always* loved us and no-one else in the entire world. Her love was constant.

But what kind of love could it have been when she was reduced entirely to spectatorhood? When she had nothing to fill her world or her thoughts, but us – our appearance, movements, words, attitudes, comings and goings? It must have been love on the sidelines, love on the bleachers, cheering or booing at the display. Every gesture noted, either appreciated or condemned, without possibility of neutrality or tolerance.

No wonder we became exquisitely over-sensitive, for only babies want that intensity of attention; to the emerging adult it is a flame which lights the fuse-wire to dark and explosive emotions, to rebellion. But rebel against what? Against someone who has, ultimately, no power whatsoever?

Let's just say, you weren't very well then, Mummy. In fact, you really were very ill, and we all had to make allowances.'

– You're mad! You're absolutely mad!

– Your mother is very ill. How dare you say such a cruel thing to so sick a person?

– But it's true, Dad.

– If it is, all the more cruel to *say* it.

I think the aeroplane has gone into a tunnel, though I know such a thing is not possible. The walls are closing in on me, smaller and smaller, as I search frantically for Good Times.

'Remember the girl at the drive-in hamburger place who saw Fred and asked "What kinda dawg is that?" and since we hoped for a free hamburger for him, we said a hamburg-eating dog. She fell for it and said, "Oh, is that right? I never heard of one before." And Nanny walking around the supermarket with her umbrella up because it was raining outside? And Uncle Arnold walking into the First National Bank of Nova Scotia and telling the manager he had decided on a merger?'

I will have to do better than this.

I can't say the true, real things any more: they are too obvious and too awful. I must keep mum, keep dumb, make up other things. For I cannot say that I was growing up and she was growing down and when we met and clashed in the middle the fallout from the explosion contaminated and distorted us. Though that is the simple truth.

'It's a question of interpretation, Mum, there are no absolutes.'

Of course there are, she informs me, Right and Wrong for a start.

Oh yes, how *dumb* of me.

13 Those in Peril

There are no Nuns on this plane. I have checked. Strange. Not that I need a Nun, only in films there is always a Nun. Someone to disapprove of any hijinks going on, someone to comfort the dying in a crash, or to smile smugly as the dawn comes as if to say, see I was right, everything's going to be *all right*. Someone to sit there sucking the end of a ballpoint pen with an airmail letter on her black lap, gazing at the sky for inspiration; writing to God.

Letters are the very highest form of communication. The pinnacle. Telephone calls with one whose voice is distorted is tantamount to talking with the dead, or making signs through the fog, and direct conversation is hampered by a welter of non-verbal material which confuses and contradicts what is being said. You cannot tear up a spoken sentence and restructure it, rephrase it, cancel it; nor can you wind back a telephone conversation to start again. In both these forms of so-called communication, you are at the mercy of time and place and obliged to say something whether you will or no. Letters are supreme. You choose when to write them. Am I feeling sufficiently optimistic, creative, relaxed, to write to my mother? No. Right then, I won't. Yes. Then I will. Simple. And the result: the right thing said, with the very right words. And even if they are *not* the right words, even if you have made the wrong gestures by mistake, don't think a letter commits you forever, whereas the spoken word will fade and disappear. The reverse is true: because the letter is written down, it is soon forgotten, like those lists we write so that we may forget all our obligations: it is the heard word which endures on the primal memory, attuned to memorize what it hears, for safety's sake. How many times has someone said to you, 'You once said . . .' 'No, I didn't . . . I would never say such a thing.' You probably did. But do people ever say, 'You once wrote . . .'? No. They read, and while the gist of it, the shape of it, remains in the mind, the actual words stay on the page, in the drawer, in the back bedroom.

But the best thing, the very best thing about the letter as the sole means of communication is that it *avoids confrontation*. You cannot have a row by letter. You can have a long drawn-out disagreement, but not a true row. The time-lapse between sending and receiving is enough for the bile to have subsided on both sides, sufficient time always passing for the hurt to have healed. As if two people could insult each other across the planet!

Or so I thought.

And so it is that while I was away at Oxford, a sort of sentimental picture of my Canadian family, with whom I exchanged letters only, grew up in my mind. I sent stylish descriptive letters about the Parks and the Colleges in the Fall, which I was relearning to call Autumn, and brief, masterful character sketches of dons and students. I said I was homesick with some conviction, because I was, though for what exactly was a mystery to me. So that I looked forward to their visit at the end of Trinity Term of my second year.

It was to be my twenty-first birthday.

'Do you remember coming to see me at St Anne's, Mummy?'

Ah, so lovely, she says, looking upward, as if the dreaming spires were visible along the almost empty luggage racks above.

'It all seemed more glorious just before you came because I was imagining showing it to you all.'

Trying to imagine what it would look like if I had just flown from Canada. When I had arrived, it was Fall and frankly there is nowhere on earth you can travel to from Canada in the Fall and be overly impressed. There are no colours anywhere like Canadian autumn.

'Spring and Summer in the University Parks and along St Giles – there's spectacle for you.'

Just like Cambridge, she says.

'You're saying that to annoy me. Cambridge is insular, flat and boring.' I say, to annoy her, and because it is part of Family Myth and Ritual that she always says that and I always reply that, and then she says,

You were born there, though, and I say:

'My allegiances are to Oxford' and then it is done.

I couldn't have forgotten she was in a wheelchair. After all, I had booked them into a ground-floor room in a hotel in the Banbury Road especially. Not that I had done well: they only stayed there one night because something was wrong, and moved to another.

'Tom had grown another foot and all your faces had changed.'

You had changed the most, she says.

If anything the wheelchair added glamour to the proceedings. At Oxford eccentricity was fashionable. People who possessed none naturally would affect some, cultivate some.

The porter renovated the defunct lift in Gatehouse just for her, so she could come up to my third-floor bedroom, to see for herself. No-one gave me away when they came to view the parents by saying, 'Oh, where's all your stuff?', for the room was virtually empty to aspire to her ideas of orderliness.

Here is Oxford, Mummy, all shimmering youth rushing about, punting and drinking champagne and Pimms and competing. And you can only gaze on from your wheel-chair. And ten, fifteen years from now, will I be . . .?

165

Tell me about the forged essay, she says.

This is more Family Legend, an old true Myth, and the telling is her favourite ritual. She grins, chokes, and grins again. Tell it *all*, she gasps.

'The previous night I found myself at a party in somebody's rooms. People were trying to impose their personalities shoulder to shoulder in two rooms, one of them a sort of kitchenette. There was loud music, chaos. It came to me just as I was darting an arm through the throng to grab a sausage-roll that I had read not one word of Dryden and was supposed to present an essay at nine o'clock the next morning, a mere eight hours from then.

'I found him giving forth in the kitchenette, dressed in a long flowing gown, waving an ivory cigarette-holder about, snatches of poetry sparkling from his great height: Anthony C, graduate, expert on Dryden. It was too good an opportunity to miss.

'Anthony, I said, I need a twenty-minute essay to read out to N tomorrow morning at nine o'clock. Upon what topic, pray? Dryden. Dryden in general, or anything in particular? Just Dryden. Typical of this place, he said: Dryden in general, Milton in general; there is no such thing as "in general" to the educated, sensitive mind. Such as your own, Anthony. Exact-ly.

'So we sat at the small blue formica table and Anthony spouted about *Absalom and Achitophel* and other, related matters. I wrote, as fast as I could.

'I wasn't the only person who thought his utterances brilliant, original, humorous. So did the crowd which gathered over the next halfhour to listen. He bridled, and swelled and became more and more eloquent as he went on. And I more and more dizzy and inebriated. But I wrote down every word, some in abbreviated form – a speed-writing which I have never been able to reproduce since.

'I went home and slept for a few hours.

'Later that same morning, I gathered up the sheets together with a library copy of the Complete Works and cycled off to Badliom College. Two other people were already waiting outside the oak door when I got there, up on the third floor.'

(My mother is there with us now, panting, squatting on the wooden landing, egging me on.)

'We sat, and without preamble, I opened up my folder and looked upon the "Forged Essay" for the first time since Anthony had dictated it.'

Now she catapults her barbed wire nails to her lips and chuckles, for she knows what's coming.

'It was gibberish. Complete and utter gibberish. No sentences, no capitals, no full stops. Only the quotations looked vaguely like English. The room was silent. The world's foremost authority on Dryden was waiting behind his large desk. My colleagues were waiting, pens poised to take notes. There was nothing for it but to read. So I did, with confidence, with brusqueness. It isn't easy to read gibberish as if it were English. From time to time there was a quotation, intact, which was like a temporary life-raft so I slowed down, looked up at the world's foremost authority and read the quotation slowly, deliberately. He nodded, sagely, and it became apparent that he had decided that I must be some sort of budding genius, one whose thoughts were somehow beyond even him. Naturally, he didn't want to give the impression that he could not follow what I was saying. Neither did my colleagues, who, taking their cue from him, were bravely jotting things down on their notepads. What? What on earth could they be writing down?

'I stopped. The don was sitting on the edge of his chair with a deep frown across his face. He sat up, slid back in the leather, and said, "Well, that certainly kept me awake" and went on, not as he should have done, to comment on my essay at length, but instead, launched into his own, obviously prepared lecture on Dryden.'

She breathes heavily, twitching her head. The ritual is done. It was well done; there were no 'almosts'.

* * *

We couldn't take her punting, Christopher and I, but we took her to watch it, to spectate it, and later, on the last day, I took her for a walk on a thundery hot afternoon down to the river to watch boats pass and to see the flowers, the very essence of Oxford: the hats and the Laura Ashley dresses passing along on the water. We stood in the hot air and watched – well, I stood behind her, behind the chair, with tears in my eyes, remembering that photograph of her and my father on a punt in the Other Place in the first bloom of their doomed love (I had been reading *Wuthering Heights* for the ninth time) just before I was born.

Then the rain started, not gradually, but suddenly. There wasn't sufficient cover under the enormous oaks since their canopies began too high, so I had to run, pushing the chair fast along the asphalt paths and cobbles, over the road to St Anne's and back to shelter. She clutched some shopping to her in terror, or in an effort to recapture the present.

Later that afternoon, with the rain still pelting at my window and them all gone back to Heathrow, I couldn't write my essay on Yeats and tried twelve times to write a poem instead. I was trying to put on paper the unsayable essence of their visit, only apparent to me. One of them, or two of them, or, probably, all of them, were in terrible jeopardy but there was nothing I could do about it, only carry on as if their visit was just an interruption; my whole Canadian side just a corollary to the present. Oxford continued, after all, unchanged, unmoved by the visit. Life settled down into a frantic normality, with little time for serious thought on topics other than Yeats, Milton, or Middle English. Open-air plays bejewelled the night-time quads, and parties gathered in the dusk and dispersed at dawn with cries of departure piercing the soft privileged air and rebounding from the crumbling sandstone faces of buildings of almost unthinkable antiquity.

Dreaming, dreaming.

* * *

Visits home to Canada entailed holding the breath and making semblances of regular life. As if nothing had changed. That summer I spent in Halifax, reading every single word Shakespeare is thought to have written, in my white room in the new house, closer to the hub of things, with the tunnel-cum-bathroom. Christopher came over near the end of my stay, having been in Russia.

'Remember Christopher's visit?'

She does, nods.

The house was heavy with Shakespeare and rent with the madness of my mother, more Lady Macbeth than Ophelia. Staying there must have been a test far worse than any which a Middle English lover ever had to undergo.

'When we had the ramp made for you.'

She must be able to motor her chair through the front door, into the front garden, to wave goodbye to my father as he leaves for work. It had become an obsession, though there was no other reason for which she could need to go through the front door on her own, since she could not safely get any further.

I remember her at the bottom of this ramp, having shouted and shouted at my father not to go to work, though he had to, it was not optional. Christopher and I are standing behind her. I have tried saying comforting things to her like 'Christopher and I will keep you company' and 'Please keep your voice down' but to no avail. She continued to scream and shout and cry as the car slid backwards down the drive and away. Tom had muttered to us that she always 'carried on' like this nowadays, and had gone downstairs to play a record. But I was thinking, what on earth will Christopher think?

— Mummy, come in now; he's gone.

— No, I will wait here.

— For how long?

— FOR EVER!

* * *

And then letters, letters, letters. Her letters to me had that stilted quality of dictated but personal material, couched in all-too-grammatical language. The spelling and punctuation varied as to who was writing for her, but the fact that she was not telling me the truth about anything was abundantly clear all the time.

Nothing ever went wrong. Everything went smoothly. Especially considering the weather, the age of the dog, the problems with the car. The dog continued to prosper, and amused the family with his now ageing antics. Tom won prizes at school, chess championships in outlandish places. They made trips, without incident, to California, Hong Kong, places 'like that'. Some were for conferences to which my father was never allowed to go without her (who will look after me? My mad sister?) and some (those to the Far East) for alternative medical treatment.

My father was very 'busy as usual', the acupuncture was not wholly unsuccessful, as I could imagine. Could I? I had only her word to go by and it was a constrained word, a dictated word. As if these letters would one day be legal evidence. I am quite well at the moment, she would say. She should have said, perhaps, that there were no current complications to add to the misery of her deteriorating condition.

I shouldn't really have been surprised when, the night before my first Final Examination at Oxford, the pay phone in the wrong building at St Anne's was for me, and it was my father telling me that Nanny had died that day. It was my birthday too. My mother hadn't mentioned that she was ill; she had been 'getting older as we would expect', the last time she had been mentioned at all.

Letters continued through my teacher-training, and on into my first teaching post in Reading: still they all prospered, still things were As Well As Could Be Expected, especially considering the weather and the fact that now Tom had left them and was living with me in England, he hardly ever wrote and did not want to visit.

Love, Mum and Dad.

Then there was a gap.

No more joint letters: no more love Mum and Dad; it was schizophrenia complete. Letters from her and letters from him, on office stationery and sent without her knowledge. It became clear that since Tom had left and come to live with Christopher and me, there was absolutely nothing to prevent the break-up of the world's most inexplicable marriage and it was coming apart at the seams with seismic eruptions.

It seems to me that a surprising number of unhappy couples get to the point where it seems to them that the only solution is that one or the other of them must die, even without the obvious disaster of serious illness. In the case of my parents, it was not just the participants who thought so, for the family doctor agreed, and threatened my father with imminent fits, seizures, strokes and heart attacks if he did not leave and end the alliance. Your children can predict this for two decades, but let the family doctor say it once, and he need not say it again.

I only regret that this wondrous medical man, an Englishman as it happens, did not say what he said ten years earlier.

I was there on one of my three-week visits during one of my father's 'turns', and was terrified. It had never occurred to either my brother or me that he could not *bear* it, that he had not the strength to endure it for ever. We could see an end to our own suffering, for obviously the term of our sentence was shorter than his, but once Tom had left them, they were sentenced to each other without distraction for ever.

The door of the understairs bathroom, invented from the now bricked-up tunnel whose purpose had never been fully understood, was jammed, and my father was inside. We had seen him go in. It was not locked and could be moved about an inch before some obstruction stopped it.

– Are you alright, Dad?

No answer.

– Tom! Come and help! He emerged, with his friend, the one with the parents who . . . and between the three of us we managed to break down the door, literally tearing it from its hinges.

My mother could see us through the adjacent arch to the sitting room and was screaming with rage and panic. It was a mixture of 'How dare *he* be unwell' and 'Please God, don't let him die'. She was trying to throw herself onto the floor to come and see what was happening because we could not stop to tell her. There was no time; we had no way of knowing until we could get to him, whether he was breathing or not. Meanwhile my mother lost what little control she normally exercised, and went completely and utterly insane, there on the floor, six feet away from the first aid work.

We could not get to him until the door was away. Tom's friend seemed to regard this sort of thing as quite normal and was simply going about his part in it with an amused sort of perseverance. The damned door must have been solid maple and about four inches thick: the original outer door to the original tunnel perhaps.

He was unconscious, on the floor, and stiff. He was in a standing-up frozen stance, as if interrupted rather than collapsed. Ashen grey of face and blue in the lips. We dragged him out and across the floor, slapping his cheeks, and waiting for a sign of life in the long hairs of his nostrils. To the sofa, and up on to it. This was a mistake, for now my mother's screaming was closer and hampered us from calming him as he came round. Tom's friend was dialling a number he had read off the noticeboard, presumably the doctor.

– Dad! Dad! Speak. Say something.

Tom was shaking him and when he came round he was confused and asked who was screaming. Had *he* been screaming?

– No, not you.

* * *

Nothing was ever the same again. Some things you can take for granted for decades, until you see that mortality is ubiquitous.

Catatonia was the name of these 'turns' and they were a reaction to intolerable stress, to peril. He had finally stopped smiling, and so did we.

Thank God for the corporeal, the visible, the manifest. For without these obvious signs of the peril in which my mother put everyone who cared for her or came into her orbit, people would have said that my father was some sort of devil for leaving her, for putting her into a lavish nursing home for the rest of her life. But thanks to the physical, the visible, the manifest, they saw it as the act of survival it was, the no-choice move you make just before the Endgame.

Everyone except my mother, of course.

Who raged and raged and harassed and harassed for eighteen months until there were no moves left to her save one.

Dear Jane,

Your mother is tolerably well, all things considered. To make no bones about it, she has had terrible trials what with the Divorce and she had to change to another Nursing Home, and your father has remarried a Woman. You know that of course. Well, there is a light at the end of the tunnel, you see, because we have managed it – found a Nursing Home near to you in Reading which will take your mother in August.

She has no friends here, as you know, except Mrs E, and they are at loggerheads just now, and would so much like to be near you, the apple of her eye, her own dear daughter. And to see Thomas sometimes when he is not too busy with his Mathematics at university. I hope you will help us with a little problem – your mother is not Allowed to travel unaccompanied, because of her Condition. We hope you will be able to come and Escort her. Of course your mother will pay

173

for the flight and you can stay here for up to three weeks, and make a Holiday of it, if you would like.

We are not naturally forcing you to do anything you don't want to do. You can lead a horse to water, eh? Reply soon we are waiting.

Love and kisses from your
Aunty Gloria
(and Uncle Arnold sends love)

14   Terminus

Dawn comes. As it usually does. First the darkness greys around the edges, and begins to scatter. The curve on the sides of the porthole window distorts and scatters into lines, a distortion which has given rise to many false 'sightings' of UFOs on aircraft. I am not deceived. The Creator played this joke only once: no joke is funny twice.

I do not dare to hope for breakfast as the trolley makes its laborious journey to the back, and to us. I just hope that my mother will eat so little that I might scavenge.

Now a definite orange is seeping through the bottom of the glass, and now a yellow, low light which catches at the bending thighs of the Trained One and the Walloped One; the light catches on the maroon like the negative of the sunrise. The sunrise to those who have not slept in anticipation of it is not settling, glorious, or restful: it is for me unsettling, disturbing, and enervating.

This might be my last meal, says my mother, looking at her croissant.

Please, I think, let not the bilingual fare of Air Canada be the final meal of my mother.

'Could you eat this?' It is the Trained One.

'What is it?'

'A dinner rejected from last night – First Class.'

'Well, so long as it's First Class, who am I to quibble?' I look at it; it is hard to eat steak and petits pois for breakfast, but not impossible. Also, it is not really breakfast time, not really any time. Just sunny mid-Atlantic o'clock. Not *mid* Atlantic any more either, for there is land, just a stripe of it, in this blinding beginning out there.

'Do you feel any better?' I ask her, meaning, my monologue, has it improved your view of life at all?

Yes and no, she says. Where has she learnt this equivocation? I wonder. She was not wont to see two sides to anything.

I eat my playboy's breakfast in silence. My mother's breakfast, apart from the croissant, has not needed to be puréed, for it seems to be porridge. She requests a pill, a particular pill. I find it and wonder how to administer it.

In the porridge, she says, crush it with the back of a teaspoon first.

'What is it for?'

You don't need to know that, she says.

Oh, the things I never need to know.

So I crush the white tablet between the back of a plastic spoon and the white plastic of my tray. I spoon the adulterated porridge, as if to a toddler. My mother seems to have shrunk during the night. Is this possible? Do people shrink and swell according to their importance?

There is no flesh on the hands or wrists: none at all. Just liver spots and freckles on white, papery skin. When her arms wave about with the strain of chewing, it is as if turquoise crêpe streamers were undulating in the breeze.

The sun is bright now, blinding, and the messages are coming over the intercom from the, now sober it seems, pilot. It is about our estimated time of arrival, and weather conditions in London, England. The trays are collected, the 'tables' snapped back, seats readjusted. The Trained One and I take my mother to the toilet and I note that the skin is hanging from her inner thighs and calves like a pair of over-large nylon stockings. And then, all too soon, we are extinguishing and tightening in preparation for the descent.

176

The pilot, in one last attempt to amuse the passengers, dips and swerves over London for our perusal. How do you like it, folks? Shall we stop here, or go on to Istanbul? I like it well, thank you: rumoured to be the deepest green in the world, bar Ireland, this, with the reddest rows of brick back-to-backs anywhere; first out of my window and then the one opposite as mine fills with bright early morning sky.

Now would be a good time, says my mother, in a gruff, unslept voice.

'For what?' Gripping my seat, runway visible now.

To go, she means, time to go.

No, it would not. It must be very hard to get a corpse through immigration and customs. This is my mother, officer, just deceased. Doesn't look like the photo? What do you mean, neither would you if you were dead. You have to make allowances. Purpose of her visit? Ascent to Heaven: just in transit, business and pleasure.

I hold her papery hand, not too tight lest it snap.

When your life flashes before your eyes, it is not in order to be prepared for death; on the contrary, it is to review all previous procedures to see which one might be appropriate for this emergency. My mother and I had just run that tape, slowly, so only the sky and telegraph poles and trees and cement of the runway flashed before our eyes.

And then the interminable roaming around that the plane does, as if looking for its long-lost auntie on the runway. Don't remove your seat-belts, don't stand, wait, said the Trained One over the intercom in a bored voice, as people did just that, standing, stretching and sitting again, sheepishly.

'Not seasoned travellers, like us, Mum. We know when not to jump the gun.'

Roaming and roaming around. Revving and de-revving. The Steward is approaching.

'There's an ambulance waiting for you on the runway. I'm going to take you off first. Are you ready?'

'No. We're obeying orders and sitting tight.'

'I didn't know you had it in you.'

Is it a Red Cross? my mother wants to know of him.

'No, I'm not cross, no.' He smiles sweetly at her, lifting down our hand luggage from above, where we shouldn't have put it. 'Got yer drugs?' he winks at me from above.

There is not a spasm of panic from my mother, as he tells us that there will be no winch this time – he is simply going to carry her down the gangplank. Fireman's lift will be the safest, he says. She does not even react.

I should be grateful for this. I drape a coat over her legs for discretion, as the hatch opens and the Steward swings her up and starts out with her, surprised at how little she weighs. I should be pleased as her head hangs limply between his shoulder blades, her arms dangling like a corpse or someone exhausted.

But I am not. If she is not afraid, has no fear of falling, this is a bad sign: no fear, no hope. She has resigned herself to something, and I dare not even think what.

The air is bitter here compared with Halifax or Gander, and the smell of grass, though there is none to be seen anywhere, is strong.

'Hurry up'. He is waiting for me at the bottom of the ramp. I run to catch up, the Everest bumping against my legs painfully, and we start out, in a fairly strong wind, for the Red Cross Ambulance standing about a hundred yards away on the tarmac.

I had planned to take a taxi. Gloria had planned otherwise. Two men in what look like Salvation Army uniforms come to help us.

Gloria is right, for once; my mother is laid down on the stretcher-bed in the back of the ambulance and strapped in and is obviously relieved to be prone, after twelve hours of sitting. Our suitcases appear, as if by magic.

'Customs?' I ask the Steward.

'Taken care of.'

'Goodbye, then, and thanks. Will you say thank-you

to – to the one who is a trained nurse, for me?'

'You mean Charlotte?' My mother's name. Dizzy now and confused with lack of sleep, I climb into the ambulance and we set off.

Home, we're Home, she is trying to say. Yes, I say, indeed, Minis driving on the left, double-decker buses, the lot. Radio One on in the cab, in front. One of the men is riding with us in the back, sitting next to me on the hard, leather-covered bench beside her bed. He is talking about football hooligans, and my mother cannot follow what he means. He tells her not to talk, to conserve her strength for arriving. He seems to have read something on her illness. He has tea in a beaker with a drinking-spout. She moves her head to the side, and since she is up on a level with the glass, she can see out, and groans with pleasure.

As we near Newbury, I start to doze and the Red Cross man prods me. He prods me painfully and I resent him. I had planned to phone my husband from the airport. There had been neither time nor opportunity. I feel as if we have been abducted.

'Hoe-um, hoe-um' my mother is still moaning.

Home is where you know the code, and the nuances of the code, where you shed a tear with others over Land of Hope and Glory, where your eccentricities go unnoticed, where you know at a glance where someone fits in and whether they mean you harm; where you have something in common with the commonality of people; where you can name the trees and a few border plants; and where the public buildings are recognizable by their shape. You can pass there, anonymous.

Unless you are black.

Or disabled.

Or my mother.

We leave the A road, leave the B road, and turn down a track and crunch over the gravel of an avenue of lime trees towards a large brick house, the Elms Nursing

179

Home. I should have come first and visited it. I shouldn't have left it all to Gloria.

Why should I have? This isn't *my* idea.

'Lovely. Lovely to meet you, Mrs Wells.' It is a massive woman, the Matron evidently, in tweedy civvies, sensible shoes and a hair-style suitable for all occasions. 'I'm sure you are going to be very happy with us.'

We are surrounded by uniformed nurses, a gardener, an idiot, several patients, all in their nineties, all shivering slightly in the wind. The ambulance men are calling for order. Quietly, unseen, I re-erect the Everest and lock it open with kicking, willy-nilly, here and there. Like the mother who brings her daughter to the door of the birthday party, I would like to dissolve into the background now and leave her to make her own way.

Be a good girl, now, won't you?

There are steps, steps, bloody steps everywhere. It is an old house, not a purpose-built Nursing Home like the one she has come from. My mother is shouting instructions about her luggage which no-one, not even I, can understand, and waving her small black box with the nursing badge in it at the platoon of nurses, who smile questioningly, tolerantly I hope.

'You'll be able to keep an eye on her here. Much better for you,' says a nurse who is accompanying me up the second flight of stairs to Mummy's room, with the suitcases shared out between us. Should I have tipped the Red Cross contingent? Will they be given tea in the servants' quarters?

'So nice for you. Right on your doorstep, almost.' Ah, they know my address then, do they?

'Why have you put her on the top floor, for God's sake?'

'There's a lift.'

'I know, but she won't be able to operate it.'

'Matron says her sister was most particular in her letter about the *size* of the room and the *view* and facing South and things.'

'Oh God, all the wrong things.'

* * *

I refuse to go into the room until the tiny lift door has opened. If my mother is to accept the room, she must be the first to enter it, to colonise it.

'A nice bath . . .' Matron is saying, as she pushes the Everest out of the cage onto the corridor carpet. I can see terror brewing in the chair, white-faced, and about to shout.

'Ah, Matron, my mother is afraid of tottering in the bath and probably would be better off with a bed-bath for now.'

'Here we have proper baths with modern equipment. She will be quite safe with us. Nothing so restorative . . .'

She is pleased with the room: she doesn't close her eyes, say a rude word, or collapse at any rate. There are not enough wardrobes; she needs two, she says. And she must have 'close covering' which I work out, at great mental exhaustion, means wall-to-wall carpeting. The Matron, with unexpected co-operation, says that the gaps around the three edges could be filled in with some carpet tiles the gardener has acquired. Home *is* the place where your eccentricities . . .

At this point my mother indicates to me that no gardener is coming into her room with carpet tiles, which I translate to Matron, who says that of course he will not, for the garden is his domain, and they have in the grounds a boy of Limited Mental Ability who can lay carpet tiles a dream.

Or am I hallucinating all this? Is it really happening – no, it's too ridiculous. An idiot close-covering the room of my mother, who is still surely in Canada. At least she should be sound asleep by this time, having been awake, like myself, virtually forever. Asleep, abroad, awake, remonstrating. How can she keep it up?

The crowd is thinning, the Matron leaving an auxiliary to 'put her to rest for a bit before tea' and making arrangements for Communion to happen in this very room at ten tomorrow morning, courtesy of their very own peripatetic priest.

No, I'm dreaming.

Do priests do that? Fuller-brush suitcases full of the

Host and the Bread and Wine? Going from room to room like the impoverished flute teacher? His ring, kissed by a hundred old ladies in the privacy of their final bedrooms, blinking in the sun on the handlebars of an ancient bicycle?

A bit far-fetched.

Not at all. Everything should come to the door of the disabled, to the very bedside. Libraries come, in talking-book form, in Large Print form, so why not the dentist with all his drills, the hairdresser with tongs, the department store: undies Thursday, furniture weekends only, the cinema (ice-creams on the windowsills), Swedish masseuses, British Rail porters to insult you, make you feel really at home. What about Pubs? Time, Madam, time!

See, though, how technology has dehumanized the disabled: nobody needs to make the ultimate sacrifice of themselves any more.

'Sorry, she doesn't want to go to bed, is what she means.'

'Why not?'

'Perhaps she's too tired.'

'I don't understand.' Of course you don't. You are only a sixteen-year-old girl in brown and white checks, no doubt the lowest order of checks around here, doing a little part-time work, perfectly healthy. Why should you understand?

'I'll deal with it.'

'Matron said I was to see 'er inter bed.'

'Okay, do it.' No – that's not fair, the poor girl is standing ready to take my mother under the armpits in the normal fashion to undress her on the bed, and is terrified at the Midas expression in my mother's eyes. Any minute now she will run away in terror.

'What shall we do then, Mum?'

Unpack all my things, put them in the wardrobe and everything else arranged, she says, never shifting her gaze for one minute from the terrified girl.

'I'm too tired now. You're too tired. I can't. Surely it can wait until tomorrow, can't it?'

Then I'll have to do it on my hands and knees, she says.
'No, you won't.'
AYYYYWEEEEL she screams. The girl turns and runs.
'She'll get Matron, Mum. She'll set Matron on you.'
But I am too tired to argue and start unlocking the cases.
Ring room service, she says, and order a meal.
'It's not a hotel, Mum, I don't think I can do that.'
CAN. YOU. DO. A. GODDAMN. THING. FOR. ME. THEN. she
screams.
'I have just flown thousands of miles for you, half of
them *with* you, and stayed awake all night talking to you
and brought you here and *none* of it was my idea . . .' so
that *I* am shouting when Matron comes in with two burly
checked ones behind her.
'Now, Mrs Wells, let's have no more nonsense. Into
bed with you and have some rest.' She stands there,
arms akimbo, her tone of voice commandingly different.
There is a particularly English way of being politely
brutal which is given to nurses alone. My mother had it;
now she has the other end of it, for there is no good
taste about it: they simply womanhandle her into bed.
My mother and her naughty friend Beryl surely did
this: bundled some old dear into bed against her will
and then ran off giggling and mock-gagging at the
stench.
But the tone of Matron's voice brings home to me a sad
fact about the place we are in: most of the inmates are
elderly and demented.
The Matron addresses me.
'We shall find a way of understanding your mother. It
is only a matter of time. We manage to communicate
with the deaf and the blind and the mute here. Nothing is
too difficult for our trained staff. But in the meantime
we must make our best efforts to do what is best for your
mother's health, even if it seems to be against her will.
Otherwise we are not doing our duty.'
Duty? My mother's *health* – she has none. The
Matron examines my blank and puzzled face, her eyes
trace the horizontal wiggle of my lips.

'We must never, never collude with the patient's self-destructive urges' she sums up.

'Self-destructive?' Has she read my mind or hers?

'People as ill as your mother are bound to have such thoughts. Even good Christians have moments of weakness. We are here to see that she does herself no harm and will go to great lengths to protect her from herself.'

Oh boy, now my head is spinning. This is no Mickey-Mouse Headmistress, no pseudo-Sergeant Major after all; but a shrewd woman. If the patient cops it, goodbye the hefty fees. But she need never put it so crudely, even to herself: she is making a business out of the noblest of human endeavour – and the images of Florence Nightingale and Mother Teresa and all those who do it or did it for Love cannot detract one jot from the fact that she is doing it for Money. And in fact, she is probably better than most women put in positions of power – for she agreed to my mother's ridiculous requests about carpeting.

We can do without this economic-Christianity, though, this sense of Duty, which will systematically rid my mother of any individuality, any possibility of happiness; in short, which will institutionalize her.

'Thank you, Matron. You instil confidence.' Though not in me. 'I will sit with her until she is asleep, if you don't mind.'

The womanhandlers and their leader leave.

She is lying, her breathing laboured from the discreet fight, looking up at the ceiling. They have pulled the pink candlewick bedspread up to her chin and smoothed it down, as one might a pile of fresh laundry.

She asks me, breathily, to close the door.

I do.

She needs some medicine to help her sleep. She is too tired now and tense to sleep without Mogadon.

'Yes, I'll find them.' I undo the packets and spread out all the bottles, packets, blister-packs, phials and even a disposable syringe, on the pink candlewick.

'It looks like I'm going to do an operation, Mum,' I say, to amuse her.

She smiles a cosy, pink smile. She is calm now, breathing carefully, consciously. The early afternoon sun is resting on her, finding her out from the high Victorian window at the other side of the large room.

I leave off the sorting of the drugs for a moment to close the curtains. The room fills with even pinker light: a rosy, English afternoon light. The wallpaper is patterned with roses, as if round the rim of a china saucer. Delicate and slightly translucent.

'Here they are. Two to be taken at bedtime with half a glass of water. How shall I do it?'

She says she needs six. Two will do her no good because she has them so often. This could be true. On the other hand, she is only a few stone in weight, so she should need fewer.

'Mummy?' She is looking away from me.

She turns to me with the Midas eyes. Am I questioning her Absolute Supremacy over Matters Medical? This question need not be asked.

It is a lovely room, she says, looking round it suddenly.

'Mummy!' She is *not* mad, she won't get away with it; I won't let her! This whimsical turning away from anything tricky.

Will you unpack my things for me, so that I don't have to do it?

'Alright, alright. If that's what you *must* have!'

Angrily, with unnecessary force, I wrench her suitcases on to the bed, scattering some of the bottles towards her, and fit the key and unlock them. The contents of the first nauseate me, not just the slight odour of urine and cheap scent. On one side of the case there are fluffy nylon night-dresses, the sort catalogues abound in, and on the other a welter of talcum powder sets, soap sets, shampoos, hair-conditioners, and the *petit point* brush and mirror set which had stared at me through her dressing-table mirror during so many rows.

Whatever I do, I must not do it in anger, I know that. I am bound to regret anything born out of the heat of the moment, and I won't be able to convince myself later . . .

Armfuls of cosmetics I load on to the dressing-table in a jumbled heap. There is a groan from the bed. Straightening up, I can see her through the mirror, crying. Carefully, I arrange them, group them, wiping away powder that has spilled on to the glassy surface of the teak veneer.

'Good?'

Lovely, she says.

A porcelain shepherdess on the window sill, next to the small bowl with the butterfly design. All these things and their histories appal me. But I am warming up now and strew the entire room with ornaments from the second, smaller case – knick-knackeries – and return to the far side of the bed for the third, larger case.

She has a few books for the shelf; dusty, much-read. A nursing encyclopaedia, a midwifery manual, circa 1950, and a few volumes of leather-bound poetry, mostly birthday gifts from me: Shelley, Housman, Betjeman, Keats, Swinburne and Rossetti.

'I'll hang your clothes now, just how you like them.' Blouses first, then trousers, then dresses, and coats. In order of length, and smoothed, not compressed.

'See? One wardrobe is enough: it's a nice big one.' I wince at my use of the word 'nice'; deliberate, appeasing. The shoes arranged in rows on the bottom. So many shoes, with their soles intact from never having been walked on, except one pair: an old pair of mine which were too sensible for me, even for school.

Why doesn't she ask me what I have decided? All these shoes in here, unused shoes. If only we could go back to a barefoot world, with no blasted Jesus saying 'Lift up your bed', and no 'sanctity of life', before such things as Ataxias stalked the earth, when survival of the weak was out of the question. Before there were shoes.

But it's not just anyone in the slight fog my tiredness

makes over the pink candlewick bed: it is my *mother*, my actual mother, not just anyone: the one who gave birth to me and carried me through the fog of '52 and saved my life.

The quadraplegic is better off: my mother is so almost alive, that is the horror of it; she can hear, see, not help reacting, and yet she cannot respond, cannot take part in life. Paralysed people with their heads intact can joke, laugh, be understood; my mother can do none of these things. It would be morally right to put an end to it, there is no doubt in my mind. And it is immoral to let her go on living a life which is almost totally suffering.

I might hurt her, I might do it badly. Killing someone isn't hurting them: it is putting them outside the range of hurt. These are just words, nothing.

My tears drip into this dark cupboard full of shoes. I know I can't do it. She knows that I can't do it. Did she know all along? That I cannot do the right thing, that I have not the courage, the selflessness, the mercy, the compassion, and not the love?

The failure is complete, and mine.

I go and sit on the bed, fingering the Mogadon.

'I'm sorry.'

For what? she asks.

'For everything.' I don't know what I want to say any more, only that I want to say it so badly.

I administer just three Mogadon, crushed, in water. She does not question the number, either way.

She chokes. I rub her back, sitting her upright in the bed, but it is not a tender rubbing. She feels ennobled by having to endure my untender administrations.

There will be . . . she begins.

'Don't talk, just relax. You'll choke again.'

A lot of money, she insists, when she dies, for Tom and me.

'As if we care about the money! For God's sake, Mummy, don't go on.'

You never loved me, she says. She is giving me another

187

chance, and if I could only get it right, everything will be okay.

'That's not true, we *all* loved you.'

A long time ago, you mean? she asks.

I am not going to cry, I am not going to cry. It's just exhaustion. I shall put on my coat, see I can; one arm here, twist it round, another arm in, pull the collar up. I can do ordinary things, and simply say goodbye and leave. I do not have to stay in this room for the rest of my life being told by my terminally ill mother that I do not love her.

'I'd better go now.' Because I have blown it again, and I always will.

Don't leave me.

Of course, I knew she would say this.

'My husband is waiting for me. He must be frantic by now.' The first time I used the word out loud.

Oh yes, she says, looking out of the window as if she might be able to point him out, looking through, and say, there he is, you needn't have worried. Oh yes, now you have a new life, she says, the last thing you want is the burden of me.

'We'll come and visit.'

When?

'I can't say just now. When we're sorted out a bit.'

When *what* is sorted out?

'Oh, please, just *let me go!*'

As I run, yes actually run, out of the room and down the steps past a pale woman staring at me in wonder at an open door, my mother's neighbour, I can just hear her shouting still at me as I round the end of the corridor on to the ground floor.

But I can't go on running on the ground floor. I have to find my own suitcase. It is probably in Matron's office, being guarded by the womanhandlers.

I 'pop' into Matron's office as I leave. You always 'pop' in hospitals and Nursing Homes. Trivial little ins and outs, nothing serious. A migraine is only a 'slight head-

188

ache', believe us, we're the Medical People, we ought to know.

Matron and the huskiest of the womanhandlers are having a slight cup of tea by the gas fire-ette on some nearly leather armchairs and give me half a look as I enter.

'I'm leaving now, but she is having trouble getting to sleep. I have given her a couple of Mogadon. I need my suitcase and to phone for a taxi.'

'Good. We'll be seeing you tomorrow? I do hope you will keep in regular contact, it does help the patients to settle in. By the way, just two things. First, could you sign this?'

I sign the confession, hesitating between Wells and my new married name which I have not yet used, confessing to being Next of Kin, for medical and legal purposes.

'And the other thing: in future, please consult me should you decide to administer any drugs to your mother.'

'Oh, I only . . .'

'Not to worry, at all. Only I am responsible now, for her health. I see that your mother is only fifty.' It seems Matron is charging me with this crime, too.

'Most of your patients are older?' Is it my fault, Matron, her age?

'The frustration' is all she says, 'imagine the frustration!' The last addressed to the husky by the fire.

'Yes.' I turn to the desk and reach for the telephone. They are both nodding, in agreement. That's settled then, frustration. Good. Fine. Simple.

'I'll phone for a taxi, then.'

The taxi stops to let the idiot boy pass across the gravel driveway for a moment and I look back up through the birches at her window with the drawn curtains, half expecting to see her thirty, fleshed out, standing holding a curtain back and laughing. Did you think this could go on forever? You fool.

The boy's heavy boots crunch on the gravel and he stops. The driver of the taxi leans out and shouts at him,

189

'Gedoutofit!' He stands where he is.

It passes through my mind that this person could be the 'agent' of whom my mother dreams, for whom she prays. He is looking past the driver at me.

Shall I be seeing you every Sunday afternoon for the foreseeable future, as we drive down the gravel driveway with hearts of lead for the statutory visit? Shall I become increasingly distraught, increasingly weary, emotional, bitchy, as I come week after week, with a box of plain chocolates, a small bottle of brandy, a jar of sweets? While you stay the same, foolish and free? Will Christopher and I gradually come to hate first my mother and then each other, planting dry kisses on each side of her bony cheek in the red plush dining-room, having wheeled her there for a change, to escape from the interminable rosebud wallpaper and the colour television?

Will Christopher ever be able to understand a single pain she causes me, a single hurt? Or will I have to go over and over it all week to get it out of my system?

The boy moves into the woods beside us with a swinging gait.

I can't remember my address. I tell the driver Left Here, Right Here, until I see my house, a mid-terraced Victorian house, much like the Lewisham 'slum' my mother so detested. She will have to be brought to see it, one day. Oh, it's *lovely* she'll say, and so near the shops, and when can she come again?

'There must be some other way.'

'I come the way you tol' me, ducks.' I pay him and drop some coins, Canadian, into the gutter outside my house.

'Sorry' I say, stooping, 'I'm ill.'

I am ill. I am sick with extended wakefulness, with lack of sleep. The subconscious is crying out for a bit of dreaming. After a good sleep, I'll see it all differently.

Christopher at last. He has the air of someone who will take it all on, all the struggle, to the end of time, as promised: an English strength, an English sadness; what can you offer worse than I have already endured?

Such a sleep I never had, so full a sleep. Sleep that cancels out reality, that turns the stars and the universe inside out and pockets them.

And in a side-ward of my dream, on the frontiers of the psyche, is a small cot wherein my mother is undergoing the final phase of her return journey. From toddler about to walk, she reverts to prone, without head control, then her limbs begin to fold into the centre, her vision separates, so that she cannot focus the eyes together; the fontanelles separate and soften. She loses the ability to speak even her strange tongue; only bawling comes from the larynx, and sucking motions from the lips. The hands curl on nothing and fold into the chest which has flattened. The knees are drawn up, the hair has left her, and bald, damp, bent in half and diminishing, she re-enters the womb of the earth, which sucks her in and closes over.

'Jane. Jane. Wake up.'

THE END

A SELECTED LIST OF
OTHER BLACK SWAN TITLES

THE PRICES SHOWN BELOW WERE CORRECT AT THE TIME OF GOING TO PRESS. HOWEVER TRANSWORLD PUBLISHERS RESERVE THE RIGHT TO SHOW NEW RETAIL PRICES ON COVERS WHICH MAY DIFFER FROM THOSE PREVIOUSLY ADVERTISED IN THE TEXT OR ELSEWHERE.

☐	99198 8	THE HOUSE OF THE SPIRITS	Isabel Allende	£3.95
☐	99248 8	THE DONE THING	Patricia Angadi	£4.95
☐	99201 1	THE GOVERNESS	Patricia Angadi	£3.95
☐	99185 6	THE DESPERADOES	Stan Barstow	£3.95
☐	99193 7	A RANGING CALM	Stan Barstow	£4.95
☐	99186 4	A KIND OF LOVING	Stan Barstow	£3.95
☐	99189 9	WATCHERS ON THE SHORE	Stan Barstow	£3.95
☐	99187 2	THE RIGHT TRUE END	Stan Barstow	£3.95
☐	99159 7	THE GLAD EYE AND OTHER STORIES	Stan Barstow	£3.50
☐	99176 7	JOBY	Stan Barstow	£2.95
☐	99222 4	THE TALE OF AN EMPTY HOUSE	E.F. Benson	£3.95
☐	99075 2	QUEEN LUCIA	E.F. Benson	£3.95
☐	99076 0	LUCIA IN LONDON	E.F. Benson	£3.95
☐	99083 3	MISS MAPP	E.F. Benson	£3.95
☐	99084 1	MAPP AND LUCIA	E.F. Benson	£3.95
☐	99087 6	LUCIA'S PROGRESS	E.F. Benson	£3.95
☐	99088 4	TROUBLE FOR LUCIA	E.F. Benson	£3.95
☐	99202 X	LUCIA IN WARTIME	Tom Holt	£3.50
☐	99281 X	LUCIA TRIUMPHANT	Tom Holt	£3.95
☐	99228 3	A FINE EXCESS	Jane Ellison	£3.95
☐	99257 7	THE KILLJOY	Anne Fine	£3.95
☐	99130 9	NOAH'S ARK	Barbara Trapido	£2.95
☐	99056 6	BROTHER OF THE MORE FAMOUS JACK	Barbara Trapido	£3.95
☐	99117 1	MRS POOTER'S DIARY	Keith Waterhouse	£3.95
☐	99210 0	HARNESSING PEACOCKS	Mary Wesley	£3.95
☐	99126 0	THE CAMOMILE LAWN	Mary Wesley	£3.95
☐	99082 5	JUMPING THE QUEUE	Mary Wesley	£3.50
☐	99258 5	THE VACILLATIONS OF POPPY CAREW	Mary Wesley	£3.95

All Black Swan Books are available at your bookshop or newsagent, or can be ordered from the following address:

Corgi/Bantam Books,
Cash Sales Department,
P.O. Box 11, Falmouth, Cornwall TR10 9EN

Please send a cheque or postal order (no currency) and allow 60p for postage and packing for the first book plus 25p for the second book and 15p for each additional book ordered up to a maximum charge of £1.90 in UK.

B.F.P.O. customers please allow 60p for the first book, 25p for the second book plus 15p per copy for the next 7 books, thereafter 9p per book.

Overseas customers, including Eire, please allow £1.25 for postage and packing for the first book, 75p for the second book, and 28p for each subsequent title ordered.